CAN'T HELP FALLING IN LOVE

LIBBY WATERFORD

ALSO BY LIBBY WATERFORD

Sawyer's Cove: The Reboot

Take Two

Take a Bow

Take it All

Take a Chance

Hot Take in Steamy Shorts: A Kissed by Romance Anthology

Take Another Look in A Kiss at Midnight: A Kissed by Romance Collaboration

Never a Bride

Can't Help Falling in Love

Can't Make You Love Me

Can't Fight This Feeling

Can't Hurry Love

Weston Reunion

Flirting with Her Professor

Her Reunion Fling

Falling for Her Ex

For Dylan

CHAPTER 1

ROSIE'S INBOX

From: Nicole Winesap <nicole@winesap.design>
To: Rosie Snyder <r_snyder@venturahospital.org>; Kate Treanor
<kate@treanorpod.com>; Lani Kalama <lani@winesap.design>;
Ophelia Winesap <o.winesap@clintonelemen.edu>

Subject: Emergency!!! Engagement party news & more

Hey you Beautiful Badass Bridesmaids!

Engagement party planning is in full swing!! Basically my parents
are taking care of the whole thing (with my input of course), but you
all MUST be there. I don't have any sisters (*pout*), but you four are
the next best thing.

I know we're all spread out and you gals haven't spent much time
together since I moved back, but I have a feeling while we're planning this party-of-a-lifetime aka my wedding you'll get to love each
other like sisters, too! And don't tell me you're too busy, Rosie—
even doctors get days off. Kate and Ophelia have weekends free,
and Lani and I will work around your schedules. You ladies rock and
I can't tell you how much it means that you're going to be standing

up there with me on the most important day of my life—the day I say "I do" to my soul mate.

Oh! I was thinking about dress colors. You all look sickeningly good in everything, but I'm leaning toward champagne pink or buttercup yellow. Text me pix if you see anything cute! Feel free to start brainstorming ideas for the shower, bachelorette, etc. I'm only doing this once, and I'm going to do it right. I know my girls won't let me down.

Kisses,
Nicole

* * *

From: Charity Shepherd <c_shepherd@venturahospital.org>
To: Rosie Snyder <r_snyder@venturahospital.org>

Subject: Meeting request—URGENT

Dr. Snyder,

Please contact me at your earliest opportunity to schedule an in-person meeting. Since you missed the last two appointments I set up, forgive the repeated reminder.

Sincerely,
Charity Shepherd, Ventura Hospital Human Resources Director

CHAPTER 2
ROSIE

I click my phone off after scrolling through my emails, wishing the reminder of Nicole's wedding was as easily forgotten as my appointment with Human Resources. What was I thinking when I said yes to being her bridesmaid? I've never been a bridesmaid before, and it's not exactly on my bucket list. But Nicole's the one friend who's stuck by me through college, med school, and beyond. She's very, very hard to say no to. It would have taken a stronger woman than me to look into her big blue eyes and turn her down.

My mind is uncharacteristically not on work when I walk to the nurse's station to grab another assignment. Instead, I'm thinking about what exactly does formal mean for the engagement party? I suspect my all-purpose little black dress won't be sufficient and Nicole's going to make me go shopping. Barf.

"What do you have for me, Carmen?"

Carmen, the floor nurse who's currently assigning patients, scans her computer screen. "Patient in 330. Twenty-five weeks pregnant, says she's feeling contractions."

My stomach flip-flops at the rundown. The other nurses tend not to give me any pregnant patients admitted to the general medicine floor of the hospital that's been my domain for two years, but Carmen's new. I remind myself that I'm a doctor—I can take care of almost anyone. Then I spot my supervisor striding up the corridor and put on an ingratiating smile.

"Hey, Ron, can you take this one? I'll owe you a favor. I really need a break."

Carmen's expression doesn't change, she just repeats the rundown for Ron, hands hovering over the keyboard.

"You're in luck, Dr. Snyder, because not only will I take this patient for you, but I was hoping you'd take a break."

I narrow my eyes in response to his broad smile. "You were?"

"Quite a long break, actually. HR's been on my ass about your PTO."

That must be what the officious human resources lady's been after me about. I've been ignoring her efforts to meet in favor of doing my job. You'd think the hospital would be over-joyed that I'm so dedicated instead of sending a pencil pusher after me.

"Look, you haven't taken a single vacation day in the two years you've worked here. I suggest you take some time off."

"You *suggest*?" I don't take vacation days because I like work-ing. I like the routine. I don't have anything to do when I take time off.

"Strongly suggest." His smile takes on an edge of steel. He's a good doctor, and a good guy, but he's also the man who signs my performance reviews, recommends me for promotions, and approves my annual bonus. "Take a couple of weeks. Rest. Go someplace fun. Recharge. Then you can come back and keep kicking ass the way you have since day one."

I look at him steadily. He wants me to say yes—I can see it in the set of his shoulders. The question is, am I going to battle him on it or give in? I think about the pregnant patient in 330 waiting for Ron to assess her and find myself nodding.

"Okay. It would be crazy to turn down a vacation, right?" A normal person would be stoked that their boss wants them to take time off. Ha. That must be why I'm deeply unsettled at the idea of Monday rolling around and me not showing up for...my life, basically. How do you play hooky from the only way you know how to live?

Ron smiles, pleased I'm not fighting him on this. He's probably just relieved that HR won't harass him anymore. "Finish your rounds, I'll see you in a couple weeks."

"A couple weeks." It sounds like forever.

"Hell, take three. Nadia Thomas just came back from vacation, so we're covered."

"Let's not get carried away." I laugh, to turn it into a joke. Ron laughs along with me. Ron has two daughters in high school and is working on getting his pilot's license. The idea that someone would resist taking a three-week paid vacation is laughable to him.

I finish checking on my patients, making sure all the pertinent details are logged into the computer. Once my virtual paperwork is done, I'm reluctant to actually clock out. I linger at the nurse's station until Carmen notices me.

"Dr. Rosenberg said you were taking some time off." She smiles like that's a good thing. Carmen's so new, she doesn't know that not taking time off is kind of my thing. "Going anywhere special?"

That stops me. I've barely been out of the county since moving back to Ventura to take this job. Before that, I did my residency in Utah, and before that, I spent my entire life in Southern California.

"I'm not sure." Maybe a vacation won't be the worst thing in the world. I know one person who will be thrilled at the news. At the risk of my sanity, I pull out my phone to text her.

I need to talk to you. Call me later?

The response comes immediately.

NICOLE

Will do! Everything ok?

Of course.

I don't want Nicole to worry. But nothing feels okay right now. I glance apologetically at Carmen, but she's on to the next thing. I give her a few last-minute instructions about Mrs. Porter and her hip fracture in 302 and Mr. Lee and his hypertensive episode in 341.

"We got this, Dr. Snyder," she says. "You're off the clock."

"Right." I nod. I'm off the clock. I'm not needed. I'm on vacation from being a doctor for a while.

But if I'm not Dr. Snyder, who exactly am I?

* * *

From: Charity Shepherd <c_shepherd@venturahospital.org>
To: Rosie Snyder <r_snyder@venturahospital.org>

Subject: PTO Status

Dr. Snyder,

Please disregard my previous email. Dr. Rosenberg notified us of your impending use of your paid time off (PTO). You've been taken off the schedule for the next three weeks. You'll begin accruing PTO again when you come back.

Enjoy your time off.

Sincerely,
Charity Shepherd, Ventura Hospital Human Resources Director

CHAPTER 3

ROSIE

When I get Nicole on the phone and tell her I'm facing three work-free weeks, she orders me to meet her the next morning to tour her recently acquired engagement party venue. Since my choices are that or staring at the walls of my apartment, I cooperate.

The next morning I drive the ten miles north to Carpinteria, exit the 101 and follow my phone's directions to Pacifica Park, a private botanical garden that opens to the public for tours and touts itself as an event venue.

I park my hatchback next to Nicole's hybrid, grabbing my purse and my phone. I get out of the car, preparing myself for the onslaught of my best friend.

Nicole is one of those people who always seems to be doing five things at once, all of them competently and in a swirl of perfectly styled hair and effortless fashion. Today she's wearing high-waisted jeans, pretty blue suede booties, and an oversized peasant blouse that on me would look like I was playing dress-up, but on her looks chic and bohemian. She locks her car, stows her phone in her vegan-leather backpack, and hugs me all at the same time.

"Thank God for bureaucracy! The hospital's probably

worried about getting dinged by their insurance company or something for overworking their doctors. Anyway, this is the best thing that's ever happened, ever!"

I laugh and wish I were half as enthusiastic as she is.

We wander up the gorgeous palm-lined promenade from the parking lot to the main entrance, Nicole's relentless positivity rubbing off on me a tiny bit. Even if I'm not convinced this a good thing, at least someone's overjoyed that I'm being forced to take a vacation.

"The first thing we're going to do when we're done here is go shopping. Then—ooh—you should take a trip! Hawaii, maybe? Or Iceland! *Everyone* is going to Iceland."

"Calm down. You're scaring the plants. Why do we need to go shopping?"

"For a dress for the engagement party, of course."

"Oh." That's happening. My wardrobe consists entirely of work slacks and blouses, like the plain black and blue ensemble I'm wearing, so I concede defeat. "Okay."

"You have to help me figure out the menu. My caterer is giving me shit about wanting to do a sit down dinner for seventy-five. I'm paying her enough, it shouldn't be a problem. I'm not having a *buffet*." She says the last word like it's dirty.

"Seventy-five people at the engagement party? How many are you planning to invite to the actual wedding?"

"On my side? Probably two hundred. Plus Ricky's side, of course. There's a lot of overlap since our families have a lot of mutual friends. But we can't leave anyone out."

Seventy-five people for the engagement party. Good God. I don't even know seven people well enough to invite them to a party. Maybe that's why I'm not the one getting married.

I sigh as she pushes open the door of the Spanish-style bungalow with the Main Office sign outside. I suppose if I hadn't on some level wanted to be dragged into Nicole's riptide of wedding planning, I wouldn't have told her I suddenly have empty days stretching out ahead of me.

We're greeted by an efficient young woman named Tessa who whisks us right back out the door and into the heart of the garden. She gives us some information on the history of the property as we walk along a crushed stone path with prehistoric-looking plants rising up on all sides of us.

"Pacifica Park's thirty-five acres were once the estate of silent film star Esme Archer. She oversaw the planting of the grounds in the thirties and forties. When she died in 1954, the garden was established as a nonprofit whose mission is to keep the garden open as a resource for the community, to preserve its natural beauty, and to maintain the thousands of species we have living here. We consider ourselves a sort of living museum."

"It's gorgeous," I say, when Tessa's commentary stops and it seems as if she's expecting a response. It *is* a beautiful day, not hot, not cold. A few puffy white clouds float lazily by to break up the monotony of the turquoise blue sky. It's Instagram-perfect Southern California weather.

It still feels weird that I'm not at work—this morning I had to physically restrain myself from calling in and checking on my patients, but I reminded myself the hospital has other doctors, and I'm not the only one who knows how to treat patients in the city of Ventura. It's not a bad day to be on vacation, honestly, walking around a paradise on earth with my best friend of twelve years as we're planning her wedding. My heart tightens with bittersweet joy.

"You're getting married," I say, spontaneously squeezing Nicole's arm. I'm not a big toucher, and she looks at me in surprise.

"Hell, yeah, I am," she says, her smile wide. "Thanks for coming with me today."

Tessa glances at her watch. "You've reserved the main lawn

for your event, but we can set up cocktails in one of the other gardens if you're interested. Why don't you explore the gardens, and when you're done, come back to the main office and find me and we can talk."

With Tessa gone, we slow our pace, walking around a pond lined by some kind of spiky-looking tree. I know nothing about plants, apparently, because I can't name anything, but I occasionally stop to look at the black labels and try to wrap my mouth around the new-to-me names. *Euphorbia ingens. Dracaena draco. Cycas revoluta.*

Nicole sighs happily as we enter the rose garden, a riot of green, pink, red, and white. These blooms, at least, are familiar to me. "This is heavenly. I'm so happy they had a cancellation. Of course, that means we're scrambling to put this on in three weeks." Nicole doesn't seem that put out by the time frame. She does love a challenge.

"I thought your parents were going to do it at their country club."

"I convinced them that this would be so much more magical. Can you imagine it at night, with strings of lights making it seem like a fairy land?"

I squint, trying to see it. Imagination is not my strong suit. I'm a facts person. But the garden would be beautiful under any circumstances, so I nod. "Pretty magical."

"But the rose garden isn't quite right. We need something smaller for the cocktail hour, and then we can move to the main lawn for dinner and dancing."

I consult the map Tessa left us. "How about something called the Palmetum?" I lead her down a path, enjoying the sensation of sun on my skin. I feel like a lizard crawling out of my burrow after a long, cold night. The sun warms me and gives me life. We come upon a grove of large palm trees, towering toward the blue sky. There are countless different types, from short and squat to tall and willowy.

Here, the ceiling of spiky green fronds filters out the sun and I shiver involuntarily. It's quiet except for the sound of birds calling to each other. Even our footsteps are silent, absorbed into the spongy earth.

Peaceful. That's the word that comes to my mind. Work at the hospital is never peaceful, not even on a night shift. There are always buzzers and beeps, people coming and going, the rattle of carts being pushed, the clack of keyboards, the constant hum of monitors and machines. I wonder what it would be like to work here, where one's office walls are formed by tree trunks and your feet are always firmly planted on rich, moist soil.

Nicole frowns. "It's atmospheric. But too small. We might have to do the whole thing on the lawn after all."

I have to agree. This place is too sacred to mar with the banality of endless engagement toasts. I have the urge to protect the trees from frivolities. I'm reminded of another grove of trees, not palms, but oranges, rows and rows of glossy green-leaved citrus trees. An orange grove was my childhood back-yard, and I took it for granted. Now I spend all my time indoors, despite living in one of the most beautiful places in the world.

Mom would be disappointed in me.

The thought is so starkly intrusive I freeze. This is why I don't do vacations. I don't like having time to think too much. My mind inevitably goes in uncomfortable directions.

I'm saved from further introspection by a cry of pain and what sounds like rapid-fire cursing in Spanish. I exchange a quick glance with Nicole, who looks alarmed, and head out of the palm grove. Just where the path splits toward the cactus garden a man in a green Pacifica Park polo shirt stands next to a wheelbarrow cradling one of his hands.

I rush up, vaguely aware of Nicole hurrying behind me. "Are you hurt? Can I help? ¿Necesita ayuda?"

CHAPTER 4

ROSIE

The injured man squints at me with dark brown eyes from under his straw shade hat. "Unless you're a doctor, I don't think so."

Though he'd cursed in Spanish, and rather inventively at that, his English bears no trace of accent and I try not to feel self conscious at having spoken to him in my limited Spanish. I'm fluent enough to converse with my patients on most medical subjects—it comes in handy at work nearly every day—but I'm aware that I'm a white girl with a mediocre accent.

"I am, actually," I say stiffly.

"A doctor?" He sounds surprised and I nod. "Okay then." He thrusts his hand toward my face and I calmly inspect the injury. He's got a puncture wound in the fleshy part of his hand that's bleeding steadily. "What's your diagnosis?"

"Ouch. Puncture wounds can be painful. The first thing you need to do is clean it well. Do you have a first aid kit?"

"We've got all that stuff in the Quonset hut." He gestures behind him.

"Is there someone who can help you?"

He squints at me again and smiles a little. "Are you offering?"

I leap at the chance to do something useful and stop ruminating. "Lead the way."

"I think I'm going to head back to the office," Nicole says. I almost forgot she was there.

"I'll meet you back there," I say.

"Do you want me to tell anybody about this?" Nicole asks the man.

"Nah, it's not that bad. You can't be too careful with some of those palms, they've got really sharp teeth."

Nicole shudders and turns to me. "You're fine?"

"Yeah, I got this, Nicole." She heads back toward the office, and we both watch her retreat, then I follow him the opposite way.

"You local?" the man asks as he tracks back through the palm forest.

I consider the question. I was born and raised thirty miles away, and live and work twenty miles away, and I still have to think about it. Have I ever really felt like I belonged in this little slice of paradise that is northern Southern California?

Before I can decide on my answer he says something I'm not expecting. "Santa Paula High, right?"

I glance at him, or rather, up at him. He's not super tall, but neither am I. The top of my head reaches the top of his shoulder. I study his face intently for the first time—dark eyes, straight nose, well-defined cheekbones, especially when he smiles. He's got soft-looking two-day-old stubble on his cheeks. He looks familiar, but maybe because he looks a lot like every other thirtyish Latino guy in Southern California. "That's right. You too?"

"Gus Cuevas. I think we had history together one year."

Suddenly I remember. World History. Mr. Sedgewick. Gus was a junior in our class of sophomores. You had to have already failed World History to take it as a junior. I'm surprised he remembers me, but then, I'm surprised whenever anyone remembers me. "Oh yeah," I say slowly. "I'm Rosie Snyder."

"Nice to meet you again, Rosie," he says as we approach a large brown building. I'd never heard the term Quonset hut before, so I'd imagined something small and possibly made out of wood, but this is a large building constructed of manmade materials. "Or do you prefer Dr. Snyder?"

"Rosie's fine." I actually *do* prefer Dr. Snyder. But since Gus met me before I became a doctor, I can let it go. "You're grandfathered in." My weak joke elicits a smile that warms his liquid brown eyes and accentuates his blade-like cheekbones.

He points to a medical kit affixed to a wall. "Here's the first aid stuff." He takes off the straw hat and tosses it onto a table covered in seed catalogs and magazines and empty coffee mugs. His black hair is buzzed short on the sides, longer on top and almost curly in front. I try to remember him from high school beyond his quiet presence in World History and come up empty.

I take a look in the first aid kit, grab a few things out of it, and then walk over to a large industrial sink and grab the antibacterial soap. "Let me help you wash it, then we'll see if it needs more than a Band-Aid."

He follows along without protest. I don a pair of gloves, then clean the wound and the hand around it. His hands are sturdy and calloused, the nails blunt and lined with dirt. The water swirling around the drain is brown with soil and blood.

"What happened?"

"Got attacked by a vicious *Phoenix canariensis*," he says ruefully.

I have no idea what that is. "Does that happen often?"

"Scrapes and cuts are a hazard of the job. But no, not usually this bad. Wasn't wearing my gloves."

"It's not that bad. No stitches or anything," I say. "Just keep it dry and change the bandage every day." Since the wound is on an awkward place on his hand, I do the honors of dabbing on the antibacterial ointment and the bandage. He holds still, calm while I work.

"What kind of a doctor are you?" he asks when I'm done.

"Hospital doctor," I say, tidying up the supplies I've used. "Basically a generalist. I work at Ventura Hospital and see whoever comes in through our doors."

"Sorry you had to work on your day off," he says with a smile. "But thanks for your help."

I'm about to shrug it off and go find Nicole, but something makes me elaborate. "I'm actually on vacation. Few weeks off from the hospital."

"You doing anything fun?"

"I don't know. My friend brought me here today. It's been nice."

"Despite the impromptu doctoring."

I laugh. "Maybe because of it, actually. I'm finding it difficult to transition out of work mode."

"Sounds like you need a beach day. Sun, sand, cerveza. No work. No computers. No patients."

"Yeah, a beach day." The words sound strange on my tongue. "I probably have a bathing suit somewhere."

Gus raises his eyebrows. "Girl, you're not a local if you're not even sure you have a bathing suit."

"I know! I'm hopeless." I try to make myself sound self-deprecating instead of pathetic.

"Listen, you live in Ventura?"

I nod.

"Me too. On the Avenue. My neighbors are having a block party tonight. You should come. Bring your friend. Or your boyfriend."

"I don't have a boyfriend."

His face lights up with a hopeful smile and I can't help smiling back. I can't remember the last time I flirted with a guy.

Med school? Maybe Nicole's right and this mandatory vacation has come at just the right time.

"Then you should definitely come. Grills get going around five, food's ready by seven."

"What should I bring?" I ask, unable to believe the words as they come out of my mouth.

He smiles again. I'm getting addicted. "You don't have to bring anything. But a six-pack wouldn't go to waste."

"Okay."

"Okay, Rosie. Hasta luego."

"Hasta luego." I'm sure my face is burning, but he doesn't seem to mind.

He turns left when I turn right to find Nicole. I can't help but glance over my shoulder halfway down the path to see if he's looking back at me. He is. I think he throws me a wink.

I smile the entire way back to the office.

* * *

"I wish I could go, if only to make sure you actually show up," Nicole says after I tell her about my encounter and Gus's invitation. "I'll just have to trust you."

"I don't know what I was thinking." We leave Pacifica Park and drive toward the beach to get lunch at a burger spot favored by the locals that's called, fittingly, The Spot.

"You were thinking, 'I'm young, I'm single, I'm on vacation. Let me flirt with a cute guy.' At least I hope that's what you were thinking."

"He is much cuter than I remember from high school. Not that I remember him that well."

"Of course he is. No one peaks in high school. I was obsessed with crimping my hair, for God's sake."

I glance over at Nicole's SoCal-perfect long blonde hair and sigh. My hair is brown and straight. And I keep it in a ponytail twelve hours a day for work.

"Maybe I should get a haircut?" I venture.

"Yes!" Nicole says way too loudly. "And please, please, please, let's buy you some clothes."

"I already said yes to the engagement party dress thing."

"Which we are going to have to do today, since the party is three weeks away!"

"How are you going to throw a party for seventy-five people in three weeks again?" The party's the weekend before I get to go back to work, back to my real life.

These three weeks I'll simply play at being someone else. Someone who spends time with my friends. Who goes shopping. Who accepts invitations from cute guys I barely know.

"It'll add drama to the event," Nicole declares. "Let me text the girls right now. We should move our planning meeting up to Sunday, since you're available."

I try to figure out what she's talking about and then remember that I'm a bridesmaid, but not the only one. Her cousin Ophelia will be maid of honor; her business partner Lani and our college friend Kate make up the rest of her side of the wedding party. Kate and I have lost touch over the years, and I don't know the other two at all.

"Sure, I can do it," I say over bites of hamburger. Why not? For once in my life, I've got nothing but time. I better fill it up before I spend too much of it thinking about how empty my life is without work. "We better get to the mall. I need a dress. And a swimsuit. Maybe some new jeans?"

Nicole squeals and claps her hands together like I've just told her she's won the lottery.

"You won't regret this," she promises.

I already do.

CHAPTER 5
GUS

I'm not actually expecting Rosie Snyder to show up to the Avenue block party, but that doesn't stop me from snapping my head up every time I hear new voices or a car roll up. I'm taking my turn on the grill, the smell of charring beef and chicken smoking everyone out of their homes and onto the blacktop on the corner that during the day serves as the parking lot for a thrift store. We hold these get-togethers every few weeks through our endless summer.

"Hey, man, I've been looking for you." My neighbor Johnny gives me a fist bump and a slap on the back. "My lemon tree is looking really good. Wanted to thank you again."

"Anytime." I'd noticed his Eureka lemon looking sorry, so I recommended an organic fertilizer and more water. Even in wet years we worry about water in this county, but citrus are thirsty. Lemons are life—the extra water is worth it. I have two in my backyard, plus a tangerine and a blood orange. I'm thinking about adding an avocado. I don't think my landlady will mind.

"How's work?" he asks.

"Same old, but good." Work at the garden usually has a soothing monotony to it, but today two unusual things happened. The first was Rosie Snyder. Thinking about her brings an involuntary smile to my face. The second thing makes my smile drop off again. Flora, the director of horticulture, announced her retirement. She's been my mentor since I was a baby gardener and the news has me feeling a little lost.

I don't say any of that because the tri-tip looks done and I'll be in trouble if I let it get tough. I go to grab a cutting board when a car door slams. I look up, as I have been all evening. This time, I'm rewarded by an eyeful of strange-but-familiar woman.

Rosie's hair is different—before it was pulled back in a ponytail, now it hangs loose around her shoulders, with a little wave in it. She's changed out of her conservative slacks and blue blouse and into a gauzy dress that shows off her shoulders.

The dress is fire engine red and she's a siren.

I can't believe she came, and I can't believe she came looking like that. I swallow hard. Maybe I've bitten off more than I can chew with this one. She's adorable, and a doctor. She was out of my league in high school and she's doubly so now.

I glance down at my shirt to make sure there's no offending meat juice or stray dirt stain.

"Rosie! Hey!"

"Hi there," she says. She might look a little different from hours earlier, but her voice is as hesitant as I remember. She looks nervous, too, clutching a paper bag so tight her knuckles are a shade paler than her skin. The bag no doubt holds a six-pack. She strikes me as the type to follow directions really well. I clear that from my head before my thoughts veer too near the gutter.

"Can I take that off your hands?" I motion to the bag and she thrusts it toward me gratefully.

"I didn't know what to get."

In fact there's actually *three* six-packs, all pricey local brews.

"Hope that's okay."

I laugh. Either she's trying too hard or she really doesn't know how to do this.

"It's perfect," I say. "I'll just stick this in the cooler, get this meat off the grill, then I'll introduce you to some people."

"Okay," she says, still soft. I want to wrap her up in cotton to match the shyness radiating off her.

I take an IPA for myself and ask her what she wants.

"Um, whatever," she says.

"What do you like?" I ask. I don't want her to take something she'll have to pretend to like in order to not seem rude.

She grimaces. "I'm sorry. I'm not much of a drinker."

"Okay, no problem. How about some lemonade?"

"Lemonade. Sure."

I grab her a glass of Tina's homemade stuff. She makes it for the kids, but I decide not to tell Rosie that. It's quick work to take the meat off and let one of the other volunteers start slicing it up. I turn the chicken and tap Johnny to take over for me.

"Okay, meat's off the grill, so I am free."

"How's your hand?"

I hold up my bandaged palm. "A little tender, but I'll be good as new soon. I was lucky to get it taken care of by an expert."

She smiles, but her pretty shoulders seem tense, and I itch with the need to put her at ease.

"Here, meet my neighbors, Dave and Poppy," I say, steering her away from the grill. "They just moved in a couple doors down from me."

Dave and Poppy exemplify the newcomers to the Avenue. It used to be mainly Spanish-speaking families crowded onto small lots between the freeway and the foothills that form the backdrop of Ventura. But with Ventura's mild weather and easy access to the freeway and the beach, the Avenue has become a mecca for millennial couples looking to establish themselves in the frankly scary California housing market.

Rosie waves at my neighbors shyly. "Dave works at Patagonia, and Poppy has her own business making..." I wrack my brain to remember what the curvy blonde does when she's not taking care of their nine-month-old, who's currently napping in a backpack on Dave's back.

"I'm a potter," she finishes for me. "Plates, bowls, that sort of stuff."

"Wow," Rosie says. "That's so cool."

"Rosie's a doctor at Ventura Hospital," I say, aware of the thread of pride in my voice, as if I had something to do with it. I think it's incredibly cool that a girl I went to Santa Paula High with is a doctor. I didn't even finish my associate's degree after four half-hearted semesters at the community college.

Whatever, this isn't a date, exactly, and I grew out of having to prove myself a long time ago.

"That's where I delivered Grayson," Poppy says, smiling goofily at her sleeping kid. "We had a great experience in the delivery ward."

Rosie nods vaguely. "That's great to hear. He's so cute."

"Thanks. We like him," Poppy says. "Hey, Gus, I wanted to ask you about the aloe you gave us. It's looking kind of sad. Maybe it needs water?"

"How often have you been watering it?" I ask.

"Like, every other day?"

"Okay, cool it with the water. It's a succulent, you don't need to drown it."

Poppy glances at Rosie. "See? Gus knows everything."

Rosie looks at me thoughtfully. "Really."

I shrug modestly, but I'm not above being stoked that they're making me look good in front of this girl.

Poppy and Rosie start talking about an upcoming art fair

where Poppy's going to sell her stuff. Dave and I head over to load up plates for the womenfolk.

As we pile on the meat, roasted veggies, and salsa, Dave asks if I want to go surfing in the morning. The best swells are usually at dawn. I don't surf as often as I did when I was a teenager, but I get out on my board at least once a month.

"Unless..." he tilts his head toward Rosie, "you're going to be otherwise occupied in the morning?"

The question stops me short. I hadn't envisioned a future with Rosie past dinner, which is about my normal MO. I am really good at living in the now. As far as I'm concerned, dinner with a pretty, smart girl, surrounded by friends and neighbors, is the ideal way to spend a Friday night. It hadn't occurred to me to try to turn the evening into an overnight visit, so to speak. I have an aversion to long-term planning, which has always done the job of throwing cold water on my relationships with women who have more of an eye toward the future. I'm not sure what kind of woman Rosie is, but I doubt she came tonight intending to get laid.

I blink. "I'll take that as a maybe, then," Dave laughs.

"Yeah, maybe." We bring our offerings back to the women and find seats at one of the temporarily erected picnic tables next to Johnny and his wife, Sophia. It turns out that Rosie and Sophia know each other—Sophia is a radiology tech at the hospital.

"I heard they made you take a vacation or something?" Sophia says.

Rosie groans. "Oh no, of course everyone knows."

Sophia laughs. "Hospital grapevine. You know how gossipy that place can be."

"Apparently they don't like the fact that I never use my PTO. So yeah, they're making me take three weeks."

"You have a three-week paid vacation?" Johnny says, raising his beer. "Fucking A, what are you going to do?"

"You should go to Baja," Sophia says. "Lay out on the beach, read all day. That's what I would do with three weeks off."

"I'd go surfing every day," Dave says.

"I'd sleep for a week," Poppy says, "but I don't think this one would let me." Grayson's awake and currently in her lap, sucking on his fist and generally being cute. "What would you do with a three-week vacation, Gus?"

On my last vacation I drove up to Portland, went to the International Rose Test Garden, stopped at a bunch of nurseries and parks on the way back, and came home with dozens of cuttings and seeds to play around with in my backyard. It had been pretty sweet, if a little lonely. No one I know would have thought coming home with a truck bed full of dirt and seeds would be a fun vacation. "Take a trip, I guess. I've never been to New York. Would love to see Prospect Park, Central Park, the Brooklyn Botanical Garden, stuff like that."

"Are plants all you can think about?" Johnny scoffs. "So, Rosie, what's on tap for your three weeks of freedom?" Every head swivels toward the brunette and she bites her lip.

"All your ideas sound nice," she says, incredibly unconvincingly. "I don't really know. I can't go to Mexico, because I don't have a passport. I don't know how to surf. New York is such a big city, I'm not sure. I guess I'll just stay home."

"Well, we have beaches here," Poppy reminds her. "You could catch up on your reading. Like a staycation."

"A staycation?" Rosie looks confused.

"Yeah, it's when you do touristy things in your hometown, like go out to eat, go to museums, shows, stuff like that. All the fun of a vacation, but you get to sleep in your own bed," Sophia explains.

"I never do any of that. And I did just buy a new swimsuit." Her eyes dart over to me. I remember our conversation from earlier and wonder if I had anything to do with her new purchase.

"I could take you surfing," I say. "You might like it."

She looks at me sharply. "You would do that?"

"Sure. I have an extra board." And a growing need to see Rosie in a bathing suit.

"I guess that would be fun."

"It's a date." I can't help my grin, and Rosie smiles back. Could this be going any better?

"I have to pee," Poppy announces. "Want to hold Grayson for a minute, Rosie?" Without waiting for an answer, she thrusts the baby toward Rosie, who accepts the bundle hesitantly. Poppy disappears and I watch, amused, as Rosie gingerly holds the baby, perching him on her lap.

"You have any nieces or nephews?" I ask Rosie, though I think I know the answer.

"Uh, no. My brother's a little younger than me. He doesn't have any kids. You?"

"My sister's older. She and her wife have a five-year-old." I might not have more than a single nephew, but with cousins upon cousins spread out all over Ventura County, I've held my share of babies. Rosie's acting as if an alien beamed down into her lap and she has no idea what to do with it.

"He's not going to start spitting poison," I say.

"I know that," she says defensively. Grayson lets out a squawk and she flinches. I can't help a chuckle.

"I thought doctors were good with babies."

"Not this one," she says a little desperately. Shit. I didn't mean to tease.

"Here, you want me to take him?" I nudge her thigh with mine, and she hesitates.

"No, I—I've got him," she says, as if she's made up her mind to stick it out, no matter what. It strikes me that Rosie would be like that—determined to see things through. It must have taken her a ton of persistence to get from our small rural town to medical school. It's not the path most people take where we're from. Most people do what their parents did, get married, have kids young. My parents still live in the tiny tract house my sister and I grew up in. I let Grayson distract me from thinking about how long it's been since I drove out to see them.

"He looks happy." I tickle the baby's chin and am rewarded with a gummy smile.

"Yeah?" Rosie glances down at the tiny bald person on her lap. "I guess he's cool."

"Babies are a lot of work," Dave says, the bags under his eyes proof. "But they've got their perks."

I always figured I'd have a kid or two. It would be rad to have a family someday, and a bigger house with more room for a proper garden of my own, maybe even space for a greenhouse. I could use extra small hands to separate seedlings and harvest agave pups. But to have kids, you have to have someone to have them with, and in the last couple of years my dating life has been more hookup, less settle down.

I glance at Rosie. What would it feel like if she were mine, if the baby was ours? I expect my heart and my mind to team up and reject the idea outright, but rejection doesn't come. Instead, a wave of longing as shocking as throwing myself in the frigid ocean at dawn sweeps over me.

I've been floating along on my own for so long I thought perhaps settling down wasn't in the cards. I watch Johnny and Sophia teasing and touching each other, married twenty-five years and still acting like teenagers. Dave and Poppy are about my age and yeah, they're tired, stretched thin as they work and raise a baby. But they're happy, and they have one cute kid.

I want that.

Am I grown enough now to make it happen? Or will I let this girl slide by me like all the rest?

CHAPTER 6
ROSIE

Poppy comes back and takes the baby off my hands, leaving me free to finish the really delicious barbecue. Gus introduces me to a few more of his neighbors and suddenly I realize night has fallen, the blacktop artificially lit by street lights and the headlights of passing cars. Today was warm as summer, but night has taken on a definite fall-tinged chill. I shiver as the party starts breaking up, people packing up leftovers in reusable plastic containers, the grill scraped down and stowed for next time.

"You cold, Rosie?" Gus asks.

I shiver again but it's not from cold. I think it's from the way he says my name. It's always struck me as a little childish, but in his mouth it sounds somehow sophisticated. "A little."

"You want to go inside?"

I'm about to say no, but he goes on. "My house is three down."

I'm curious to see where he lives, and nod.

Gus grabs a fresh beer and a plate of leftovers and waves a general goodbye to the group. I already said bye to Dave, Poppy, and Grayson, Poppy pressing a flyer into my hand with an invitation to come to a beginners pottery class she's teaching at the

Avenue art center. While the idea of taking a pottery class is kind of laughably frivolous, it's still nice to be asked. Nice sums up the entire evening. I managed to actually meet new people and not act like a total freak around Sophia, who's only seen me in doctor-mode.

Now my reward for socializing is getting to spend some time with Gus, alone.

At first glance, his house looks like every other one on the block, a small square wood-frame house probably built in the forties, with a concrete slab driveway leading to a garage in the back. There are only the street lights and the porch light to see by, but when I look harder I can see that while the house might match the others, the yard does not. Most people have a few trees, some dried out lawn, and maybe a container or two of flowers. Gus's front yard is dense with layers, covered with plants of every size and shape, from low to the ground to the towering palm tree that stands like a beacon as tall as the house. The colors all blend together in the night, but I bet by daylight it's a stunning profusion of green dotted with blooms of every color.

"Your garden is amazing," I say.

"Thanks. I try to keep the front neat, but the backyard's kind of a mess. That's where I play."

"With plants?"

"Yeah, potting, hybridizing, getting seedlings going."

"You don't get enough of that at work?"

"Work is work. This is fun."

"Huh." Work is work. That I understand. Fun? Not so much.

Gus unlocks the front door, flicks on a warm yellow light. His place is small but tidy. He's got plants inside, too, viney things spilling out of containers hanging near the windows, and little rows of cactus and succulents lined up on tables.

"Want something to drink?" He passes through to the kitchen, and I follow. He sticks the leftovers inside the fridge, giving me a chance to see the profusion of photos on the front. Lots of pictures of an adorable little boy, growing up before my eyes in one picture after another, a few with an older couple smiling at the camera. I deduce they must be his parents, since the man is an older version of Gus, with a more conservative haircut.

"Will you really take me surfing?"

He shuts the fridge door, looks at me with eyebrows raised. "If you want me to."

"I never thought about it before." It's true. But suddenly I want to go surfing more than anything, and I want the sweet, plant-obsessed man in front of me to take me.

I trust Gus, I realize, both with my safety in the water and enough to be alone with him. I may not know him well, but he has the endorsement of Sophie, he's close to his family, he's been nothing but kind to me. He's something new but feels safe. Maybe it's because I've actually known him for years that I ask, "When can we go?"

"Don't work again until Monday." He shrugs. "Tomorrow too soon?"

"I only have three weeks off," I say, "so tomorrow is perfect."

"What happens in three weeks?"

"Back to work. Back to a pumpkin, I guess."

"You're not a pumpkin." He steps forward, tilts his head as if trying to discern my genus. "You're a rose."

I blush, dammit.

He doesn't let out a laugh, but it looks like he's holding one back.

"So tomorrow, surfing." I clap my hands together like a dork. "What do I need?"

"A suit, a towel. The water will be cold, but not too bad. Some people use a wetsuit. But maybe you should decide if you like it before you invest in one."

"Okay. What time?"

"Earlier the better. Seven?"

"Seven? Okay, might as well start my staycation right."

"So you're doing it? Having a staycation?"

"Yeah. I guess?"

"That's the spirit."

I bristle at his sarcasm. "Hey, this isn't easy for me."

"You're going to do great." His voice has softened, and I don't know that I like his vague pity much more than the sarcastic comments.

"So, you ever done a staycation?" I ask.

"Sounds like my life." He grins, pops the top of his beer and raises the can up in the air for emphasis.

"Can I ask you something, Gus?"

"AMA."

Huh? "American Medical Association?"

He does laugh then. "No. Ask me anything. Haven't you ever been on Reddit?"

"Oh." I am seriously a dork. But he doesn't seem put off by that, so I forge ahead. I've been thinking about a doctor at the hospital who went on a singles-only Caribbean cruise. She babbled for a week about the hot Australian guy she'd met on the boat and had spent the entire time with.

"Sometimes people have, um, flings on vacation, right?"

I'm a little gratified when Gus chokes on the sip of beer he'd just taken. He coughs and lets out a strangled, "I guess."

"Would you—" I stop, my cheeks flaming, completely unprepared to put into words what I want to ask him. "Are you—"

He sets the beer can on the kitchen counter and steps closer to me. "Are you asking me if I want to be your staycation fling?"

I grimace and close my eyes in mortification. "Yes," I grind out between my teeth. "But if that offends you, please forget I said anything and I'll just go." This time my words are stopped by something besides my own awkwardness. Gus's lips have covered mine, and he kisses me, simple and steady, until I recover myself enough to soften my mouth under his. I kiss him back, meeting him halfway.

He tastes of hops and kisses me with just the right amount of pressure—which is to say, not too much. He's not plunging his tongue into my mouth or backing me up against a wall. He just calmly kisses me as if it's the most normal thing we could be doing right then. But it's not like he's not interested. He's calm, but focused, as if this is not only normal, but terribly, terribly important. And he's really fucking good at it.

My knees are watery and my lips feel plump and tingly when he finally draws away. I open my eyes halfway, still not sure if I'm about to leave in embarrassment or not.

"Dr. Rosie Snyder, I'd be honored to be your staycation fling," he says, a smile in his voice.

"Really?" Somehow I didn't expect it to be this easy. My body is on board, my arms almost of their own volition wrap around Gus's shoulders, a clear invitation for him to kiss me again, which he does.

This time it's less calm, but no less focused. Tongues definitely get involved, and my body starts tightening in places that don't get exercised by my treadmill runs.

"The only question is how fast you want to move, Rosie. You're in charge, here," he says firmly when we pause.

"That's good. I like being in charge," I say without thinking.

"No kidding." He's smiling as if he thinks the fact I'm a control freak is attractive or something.

I laugh. It feels so strange to be with someone I don't know very well but feel so comfortable with. I don't do this—joke around and make plans. I don't go to barbecues. I don't hold babies. I don't *surf*. Suddenly, being so far outside my comfort zone makes me feel bold. What do I have to lose?

"So if I wanted to stay over..." I trail off, testing the idea.

"Yeah, sure," he says, voice casual. His fingers trace the

joints of my elbows, slide to my hands. He brings one of my wrists to his mouth and kisses my pulse, which kicks into overdrive. One corner of his mouth quirks up. "Except I don't have a swimsuit that will fit you."

Oh yeah. If we're really going to do the whole surfing lesson thing, and a beach day besides, I need to go home and get my suit and a bunch of other things. My fantasy of being whisked away to his bedroom dies a quick, if not entirely painless, death.

I take a deep breath. Maybe it's better to get some distance, anyway. I'm not acting like myself. I might regret my impulsive request in the morning, one way or the other. Better to regret not sleeping with him than the reverse, right?

He reads my hesitation in my body language and lets me go. "No problem, Rosie. You still want to meet up tomorrow?"

"Definitely. Seven?"

"Seven. Hasta mañana," he says, after telling me which stretch of beach to meet at.

"Hasta mañana, Gus."

CHAPTER 7

ROSIE

My alarm wakes me from a hazy dream. I was lost in a forest of lush green plants with leaves the size of small cars, but I wasn't frightened. I was sure that if I just followed the path I'd get to where I was supposed to go.

Still, I don't feel all that rested as I don my new swimsuit—it's red, just like the sundress Nicole made me buy yesterday. Red is my "power color," she says, because it makes my brown eyes and hair "pop." I told her to "shut up," and bought them anyway.

Since my wardrobe mainly consists of grays and blues, which coincidentally match the colors of the hospital, I also let her talk me into a few sundresses, two swimsuits, and an admittedly gorgeous emerald green dress for the engagement party. I'm relieved to have my party outfit picked out, because I won't have to think about it a minute more.

I throw on another sundress, grab sunscreen, a big sunhat, a towel, and other odds and ends that I might need, including a full change of clothes and my makeup bag. The thought hovers in the back of my mind that I might not make it home tonight.

Other than tomorrow's obligatory bridesmaids brunch I have no plans. For three freaking weeks.

I'm not expecting Gus to spend the entire weekend with a girl he just met, but all the same, he didn't seem put off by my offer of a no-strings fling, and in my experience, men will clear their schedules if they think the possibility of sex is on the table.

There's a thin marine layer this morning, keeping the coast cool and gray while inland they're in for a dry, hot, late summer day. Gus is already waiting for me in the small parking lot next to the beach. It's pretty full already with beaters of every description. My tidy silver hatchback slots easily next to his older white pickup truck. Two surfboards that look impossibly big hang over end of the truck's bed. My mouth goes dry not at the size of the boards, but at the sight of Gus standing in the truck bed wearing nothing but knee-length board shorts.

His lack of shirt leaves what seems like acres of golden brown skin exposed. His arms are distractingly curved with lean muscle. His flat stomach is marked by intriguing ridges that disappear into his swim trunks. But most prominently of all, his chest is defined by an enormous tattoo. It's a tree, a lushly complicated snarl of branches and leaves. When he spots me and jumps down, I can see the tattoo covers his entire right side, from his right pectoral to his right scapula, even covering part of his shoulder and clavicle.

I swallow, attempting to compose myself before I get out of the car. Why did I not notice how built he was yesterday? *Maybe because he was wearing clothes*, a voice in my head whispers snarkily. That alone gives me pause. My internal monologue is never snarky. Gus works with his hands all day; it makes sense that he'd be in good shape. Still, I didn't expect him to be quite so...beautiful.

My face feels hot when I finally get out of the car and he grins at me easily.

"Hey, girl."

The "girl" slides off his tongue like a casual endearment. Like I'm *his* girl. I suppose I am, for three weeks anyway. Huh. I've never belonged to anyone before. I'm not sure if I like it or not.

He gives me a quick hug, and I'm intensely regretting my decision not to stay at his place last night. Not because I'm consumed with lust—though I am—but because now the possibility that we might have sex later today puts an awkward veil over everything we do or say. There's an unspoken expectation that things are going to go a certain way, and if I'd just gotten it over with last night, then today would be relaxed fun between two people who already know what each other looks like naked.

Gus pulls the first board from the truck, as I track the ripple of muscles in his back as he moves. I groan silently.

"What's wrong? Second thoughts?" He looks at me, confused, when I stare helplessly at the board he's offering me.

I let out a nervous laugh. "Yeah, but not about this."

He cocks his head at me. I'm not making any sense. "Never mind." It occurs to me that I'm taking a lot for granted. Just because I have no social life and am unexpectedly free for the next three weeks doesn't mean he is. Just because I'm experiencing acute lust doesn't mean he wants me back. He might have tons of plans—with other girls, even—that I won't factor into.

"You're not going to want to overthink this, Rosie." He could be talking about surfing or about the ridiculous situation I've gotten myself into.

I take a deep breath of briny salt air. Fine. No overthinking. About anything.

I grab hold of the board and lift it carefully. It takes me a minute to adjust to the length, but it's surprisingly light for its size.

He gets the other board and leads the way down to the beach. "These are longboards. Good for starting out," he explains as we stake out a spot in the sand. I set the board down flat, put down my bag and kick off my sandals. The damp sand is cool between my toes. "The first thing we need to do is check out the surf."

I try to concentrate as he describes some types of waves and some safety tips for when we get in the water. There are probably a dozen surfers already out there. After I watch them for a few minutes I come to the conclusion that surfing seems to consist mostly of sitting on your board, bobbing up and down, and talking to your friends. I can probably do that.

"Let's try it on land." He arranges his board next to mine. "The middle is the best place for your feet to be to balance. But first you have to paddle out, and then you'll try to jump up on the board when a good wave is coming at you. So let's practice paddling on the sand."

"Okay," I say, already slightly confused.

Gus points out the midpoint on his board, then in one smooth motion drops belly down, his legs together pointing to the rear of the board, his head at the midpoint. He makes practiced paddling motions with his arms, pantomiming the action. He should look silly, like a beached sea turtle, but of course he just looks cute, dammit. Then he puts his hands flat on the board, lifts his torso up and away and jumps up into a classic surfing pose, one foot in front of the other, arms graceful, eyes on the horizon.

"Not much more to it than that," he says. "Okay, you try."

I clumsily arrange myself on my board, trying to replicate his position.

"Scoot back a little, there you go," Gus instructs.

"Why is it so rough?" I ask. There's some sort of residue making the surface kind of lumpy underneath me.

"That's wax. Good for traction. Now, try paddling. Keep your legs together. Good."

We spend a while pretending to paddle and jumping up. It goes easier for me once I realize the initial motion is basically cobra pose.

"That was really good." Gus claps after I finally get the hang of the move and my feet land planted on the right spot on the board.

My thighs are starting to burn, and my sundress sticks to me unpleasantly. "Okay, I think I got this."

"I knew you'd be good at following directions," he says, grinning at me.

He's just trying to make me feel good, but it works. I smile. "You're a good teacher."

"My sister's wife wanted to try it a couple of years ago and I got her started. But if you're serious about it, you should take real lessons." I'm distracted from Gus's words as he dusts sand off his arms and chest. I'm covered in sand, too, but it just makes me feel messy. Gus looks like he belongs here, sun-kissed, ripped, sand and all. I'm just a poser trying to surf to get a guy to like me. I'm an idiot.

"Rosie. Overthinking."

I snap my gaze to his. Gus is smiling, as if he knows I'm trying to talk myself out of the fun I'm having.

"Right." If he's half-naked and comfortable, maybe I need to more fully commit—both to the lesson at hand and to the low-level lust I've been experiencing all morning. Without warning, I strip off my dress and drop it to the sand, leaving me in my new red one-piece. I feel exposed, but maybe Nicole was right about the color, because I also feel powerful. "Now what?"

I'm gratified when Gus seems to struggle to keep his gaze above my shoulders and doesn't answer right away. He finally offers me a smile full of bravado, gestures to the ocean and says, "Let's get wet."

CHAPTER 8

When Rosie playfully suggested a "staycation fling," to be honest, I thought she'd never follow through. It sounded like an idea from some bull-shit clickbait online listicle: "Top Ten Millennial Staycation Ideas." Rosie doesn't really strike me as the kind of girl who has flings.

I haven't known her that long, but I already know she's way too much of a control freak to enjoy random hookups. Maybe that's why when she'd put the idea of staying over last night out there, I'd found a way to give her an out. I'm not going to say I never put out on the first date before. But there's something about this girl. Maybe it's because I remember what she looked like as a shy, skinny fifteen-year-old in World History, but I didn't want to be something she'd regret in the morning.

She looked so cute in that soft red dress, with her eyes closed in embarrassment, I'd just had to kiss her. I wouldn't call it a mistake, exactly, but ever since I had a taste, I've been wanting to pick up where we left off. When we're kissing I actually feel more in command of the moment. She's a doctor—she's way smarter than me, way more accomplished. Then again, she'd kissed like it had been a while. That combo—

scarily competent and adorably inexperienced—it does things to me. It's like all she's had time for since high school was learning how to be an amazing doctor and at everything else she's a beginner. Including surfing.

We spend more paddling time in the water than actually catching waves, but that's normal. What's not normal is how the sight of her in a sexy red swimsuit makes me wish my board shorts offered a bit more coverage. I knew she was pretty, but now the shape of her is imprinted on my mind, and she's *hot*.

She's also a good sport, coming up from her first wipeout sputtering but laughing. And she's athletic enough that she actually got on her feet to ride the best wave of the morning halfway to shore before bailing off, back and away from her board like I taught her.

"Oh my God, I'm starving," she gasps as we finally drag ourselves out of the water.

"Nothing like salt water and fresh air to work up an appetite," I say, hoping she doesn't notice how thoroughly I'm checking her out as she wraps herself in a towel. Of course her towel is white and fluffy, while the threadbare beach towel I tuck around my waist is about as old as I am. I'm starving, too, and not only for breakfast. I wonder if she still wants to go through with everything a fling entails or if she's regretting making the offer. I tell myself I can still be her friend, even if the rest of it is off the table. But damn, it's going to be hard.

"Breakfast?" she asks hopefully. "Then more beach time?"

I pause. I definitely want to fuel up on huevos rancheros and coffee, but not for a lazy beach day. I want to be alone with her, not on a beach full of people.

She frowns when I don't answer right away. "Sorry, I should have asked if you had other plans. It's okay if you don't want—"

"No, it's not that. I'm all yours," I say, meaning it, at least for today. "I'm just wondering if..." Damn it, she had the balls to ask me yesterday, I should be able to bring it up again in the light of day. But I can't quite ask this amazing girl if after breakfast she wants to come back to my place and mess around. She deserves better than that. "I was just thinking, after the beach, you want to have dinner with me?"

"Dinner?"

"A date," I say, to be clear.

"Is this not a date?" she asks, suddenly uncertain.

Shit. I'm screwing this all up. "No, it is, I just thought…I'd like to have dinner with you."

"All right. Sounds good." She smiles. "I was worried about monopolizing your weekend."

"Nope," I say, trying to keep it casual. But I'm happy. I'll take Rosie on a proper date, and then, if it feels right, and we're on the same page, we can finish what we started last night.

It's not until we're driving separately toward the cafe that I realize how weird it was for me to lock her in for dinner. Usually I would just let the day play out, see where we were when the time came. But with Rosie, I don't want to float along, I want to make sure she's available, because not getting to see her later isn't an option.

* * *

Breakfast with Rosie is an experience and a half. I take her to my favorite place, which is packed on a Saturday morning. While we wait for a table she tells me about her friend Nicole, the bride-to-be who's booked Pacifica Park for her last-minute engagement party.

"We met at UCLA." She pushes her damp hair behind her ears. Rosie has the slightly bedraggled look of someone who's spent the morning in the ocean, but she's glowing. I see more than one guy take a second look at her, and I edge closer. Nothing wrong with staking a claim. Rosie asked me to be her fling, after all, not these bozos.

I'm thirty-one—holding her hand seems like something I would have done with a girlfriend ten years ago. But being with Rosie makes me feel like a kid on a first date. Maybe it's the fact that we knew each other in high school, and I'm transported back to those days of white athletic socks pulled halfway up my calves, peach fuzz, and my ever-present Raiders hat. I remember alternately staring at the pretty, quiet girl in World History and the clock, waiting for the minutes to countdown to freedom. School was a prison for me, keeping me locked away from the outdoors, my natural environment.

This girl, this beautiful, smart girl, went to UCLA and became a doctor. I struggled to graduate high school and didn't even finish my associate's degree. Does that matter to her? It doesn't to me.

"She adopted me," Rosie says, still talking about Nicole. "I don't make friends easily, and she took pity on me, brought me into her circle. We stayed friends, somehow, even though after we graduated she went to New York with Ricky—that's her fiancé—and I stayed in LA for med school."

"Sounds like a good friend." I catch the hostess's eye and she leads us to a table on the patio. I relax, feeling the sea breeze and the perceptibly warmer sun. We ask for coffee and identical orders of huevos rancheros.

"Nicole is amazing. She knows what she wants and she gets it. I'm a bit terrified about her wedding."

"Bridesmaid?"

She nods. "I've never done it before. But I couldn't say no."

"It'll be fine," I say, playing with a sugar packet. "You just have to get a dress, throw a few parties."

"A few? There's more than the engagement party?"

"You've got the shower, and the bachelorette. Sometimes more than one. My sister had two showers, one for friends, one for family, but then, we have a big family."

Rosie makes a face. "I'm so unprepared for this."

I laugh. "Don't worry, you're not the only one, right? I'm sure the other bridesmaids will help you out."

"We're having a planning meeting tomorrow," she says. "It's probably going to be Nicole just telling us a lot of stuff we're going to have to do."

"You've really never been in a wedding before? No sisters? Cousins?"

Her expression tightens. "Actually, I don't have much family at all. Just me and my brother, Jake. He's a mechanic. Our parents are dead," she says the last part in a rush, as if to get it over with.

"Oh, I'm so sorry." I don't quite know what to say besides that. My parents and I aren't always on the same page, but I can't imagine them not being there. Even if they weren't, the family I've got in Ventura County alone would overflow this entire restaurant if we all tried to pack in at once. Our meals are delivered before I can fumble for something meaningless to say.

"Thanks," she says generically to me and the server. Neither of us knows how to break the awkwardness. We take bites of our meals at the same time, chew in silence.

"These are really good," she says, mouth still half-full. "Hey, how's your hand? The salt water didn't bother it?"

"Nah," I mumble, too busy enjoying my own meal to make a full reply. Between the surfing lessons and the self-control I'm exercising trying to keep my hands off her, I'm freaking starving, and haven't thought about my punctured palm once.

"I'll check it again later and put on a fresh bandage."

Later. I like the sound of that, and I grin.

"Hey, man, what's up?" My friend Enrique greets me on his way to a table. I rise and give him a one-armed hug. He glances curiously at Rosie, so I introduce them quickly.

"You been surfing, man?" he asks.

"Yeah, we caught some waves."

His eyebrows shoot up as he looks over at Rosie. "You surf?"

"Not really. Gus gave me my first lesson today."

"Nice. See you around, I hope." He joins his crew at a nearby table and I turn back to Rosie.

"Do you know everyone?" She smiles. "You're like the mayor."

"Feels that way sometimes, but nah, I've just been around so long. I moved here after high school so I'm an old man now."

Maybe I sound more defensive than I mean to, because her voice is soft. "I think it's nice."

"Why did you move back?" I ask, wanting to know everything.

"It was kind of an accident. I spent most of my residency in Utah, and when this job came up a couple of years ago, I thought it would be good to be close to my brother, be back in California, and I got it. Nicole moved to Santa Barbara from New York around the same time, set up her design business. I guess we're all grownups now, even if I don't feel like one most of the time."

I smile at her, what she said echoing my very same thoughts. "Are you in my head right now? How did I get to be thirty-one? I still feel like I don't know what I'm doing half the time. I thought we were supposed to have everything figured out by now."

She laughs, the sound as pretty as a wind chime. "Tell me about it. My problem is, I had to grow up early. I feel like I missed out on being a teenager sometimes."

"Well, as someone who still feels seventeen, let me tell you, it's not as great as you might remember."

"Still, I never broke curfew, or got drunk at a party, or played hooky from school."

"I'm shocked." Rosie is the least likely person to play hooky I ever met.

She pushes my arm playfully at my sarcasm. I like it when

she touches me. I'm definitely feeling seventeen again, or at least as horny as a teenager. I think about how far away dinner is, about how I wanted to take her a proper date. I think about how all she's wearing under her little sundress is a damp swimsuit and I wonder what her skin would feel like under my palms. She'd taste like the sea—salty and sour. Suddenly, I'm craving something savory, specifically, her skin, her mouth. Her pussy. I imagine how she'd look spread open underneath me, and I get goose bumps.

"So what's next on your staycation agenda?" I ask, wrenching my mind from the gutter.

She pushes away her empty plate—she ate faster than me, which is saying something—and sighs. "I don't know. I'm so terrible at this. I feel like I'm playing hooky from work but they don't even want me there."

"That's not true. They want you there, but they want you to have a life, too."

"I guess." She doesn't look convinced.

"Listen, you can do anything you want today. Anything. And you aren't seventeen, thank God, which means you can do grownup things."

"Grownup things?" She looks at me through lowered eyelashes and I regret my choice of words.

"Like, uh, drink and rent a car." What else can I suggest that isn't sex-related? "Eat dessert first."

She licks her lips. The blood in my head rushes south, making my brain even more useless. "Dessert sounds good."

"Dessert. Yeah. They have good beignets here."

"Gus."

"Yeah?"

"I don't want beignets."

"Okay. Waffles?"

"I don't want waffles or pancakes or cinnamon rolls or muffins."

"What do you want?"

"You said I can do anything, right?"

I nod.

"I want to go back to your place. Specifically, your bedroom."

She doesn't have to spell it out any more. I bolt from my chair, pulling my wallet out and dropping more than enough to cover the bill. There's no way I'm waiting for change. "Let's go."

CHAPTER 9

ROSIE

Gus's house looks much the same by the light of day as it did last night—shabby but loved—but the garden is even more spectacular than I expected. I'd been growing steadily more nervous on the drive over, even though logically I'll feel better after we just get it over with already, hopefully in more ways than one. Still, I basically told him I wanted to sleep with him. We're driving here with the purpose of hooking up. It's just not...me.

Maybe that's why it feels so good. I hadn't realized how sick of myself I've become, existing solely to work, viewing anything that takes me out of my routine with suspicion and annoyance. I need this shake-up, and now I'm as effervescent as a can of bubbly wine that's been similarly shaken.

"Your garden is outrageous." I pause to stick my nose next to a big red hibiscus and inhale. It's about the only thing in the yard I recognize well enough to name. "What's that gorgeous thing?" I point to a plant with multiple coral colored blooms coming from intricate bulbs embedded in the soil.

"*Haemanthus coccineus*," he says. "South African. The one next to it is a relative, but it's not going to bloom for a while yet."

"And you planted all of this? How long have you lived here?"

He leads me up the walk to the front door. An unfamiliar-looking bush with leaves soft and feathery brushes against my bare leg. The air smells like living things.

"Six years now, I guess. Lived in a little shack with some friends before that. When I got my job at Pacifica Park I got this place." He unlocks the front door and I follow him into the space where I kissed him last night. Or he kissed me. Where we kissed each other.

"I sort of thought if you worked in a garden all day, you wouldn't want to be in your own yard in your downtime."

He tosses his keys into a wooden bowl on a coffee table, goes through to the small kitchen. "The gardener's yard has no flowers? Hey, you want anything to drink?"

When I shake my head no he changes direction toward a small hallway, gesturing for me to follow. "Nah. I couldn't bear to leave it what it was—crabgrass and a dying eucalyptus. My landlady doesn't care what I do, so I started with a few lady palms and never stopped."

"Did you always love plants?"

"I loved being outside. Anything that takes me outside is all right by me—gardening, surfing, hiking. I don't like being trapped inside."

"You'd hate working in a hospital, then. Sometimes I forget what fresh air and sunshine feel like."

"That's too bad. You're no hothouse flower, Rosie. You need sunlight, too."

He leads me to his bedroom, and my eyes widen. He wasn't kidding about not wanting to be trapped. This room is different from the others. The windows are oversized, and a sliding glass door leads to the backyard. I look up to see a large skylight.

"Wow. Was it like this when you moved in?"

"I told you, my landlady doesn't care. I put in the door a

while ago, and the skylight last year. I like feeling like I'm outside, even when I'm inside."

There's not much else in the room besides a large bed with rumpled blue sheets and a dresser with a few photographs and a Pacifica Park ID badge.

And light. Lots and lots of sunlight. My visions of an intimate tryst disintegrate. Not sure what I was expecting inviting myself back here for a midday quickie, but I hadn't pictured it being quite so bright. My already limited bravado fades in the face of Gus's sun-drenched bedroom.

"Hey, you okay?" He looks around, as if seeing it through my eyes.

I drop my bag on the floor, suddenly remembering I'm sandy and salty, my hair tangled from the ocean. I can still taste the onions from my breakfast. This is the least organized I've ever been about sex in my whole life. I've never slept with anyone without thoroughly showering, coifing, dressing with care first. But Gus isn't like the other guys I've slept with.

We might call what we've been doing dates, or a fling, or whatever, but he feels more like a friend than anything else. Of course, the friend thing only goes so far, since he's really hot, and I definitely want to have sex with him. I can let go of the "having sex for the first time in a brightly lit room" jitters thing.

"I'm fine," I say firmly. "Just wondering about your neighbors."

He grins. "Don't worry, they can't see a thing. I've done extensive research." He lowers the blinds on the windows anyway. "Seagulls sometimes land on the skylight, but other than that, it's cool."

I look through the sliding door, and he's right, I can't see any windows belonging to other houses between the backyard's high fence and the eucalyptus trees that line the backyard.

"Okay." With the blinds down the room's dimmer, but still

bright and airy. Everything's going to be visible. He's already seen me in nothing more than a swimsuit. Still.

"Are you sure you want to do this, Rosie? Because I don't want to be something you're talking yourself into because you think it's good for you."

I'm a little surprised that after two days he knows me well enough to make that astute comment, but I'm even more surprised that I reject the notion entirely. Getting laid probably will be good for me, but that's not why I want this. I want this because I want *him*, and I've gotten so little of what I've wanted in my life. I want to taste something that's just for me, just for pleasure. Not because I have to advance to the next level, to drive myself forward, to leave my guilt and sadness behind. This isn't about forgetting something terrible. This is about reaching for something good.

I don't answer him, just get close and nestle myself against the flat plane of his chest. He wraps his arms around me without me having to ask, and it feels so good I could cry. I can hear his heart beat through his ribs, through his thin white T-shirt. It thumps loudly, reassuringly, reminding me that Gus is alive, thriving. He's healthy and strong. He doesn't need me to heal him. He's perfect.

Slowly, I tilt my face up and meet him for a kiss. It's only our second time kissing, but we slip into it easily. His lips are familiar, thin lips that caress mine, a confident tongue that suggests, not invades.

His kisses take me out of my head and bring me into my body. I feel grounded in a way I rarely do, as if I'm connected to the earth through my flip-flops and the wood floor of Gus's bedroom, as if being with him, in this room he's made as close to sleeping outside as he can make it, has rooted me.

If my feet feel planted, the rest of me feels as if I'm blooming, opening up under the warmth of his attention and careful kisses. I'm warm and alive, my breasts suddenly heavy as I press them against him more firmly. With each sweep of his tongue against mine I feel an answering tightness between my legs.

Gus gently walks me backward to the bed and we sink down onto it together, his arms still wrapped around me, my hands around his waist. We kiss until my head feels fuzzy and my lips chapped. I unwind myself, reaching up to touch his short hair with my fingers. It's as soft as it looks, untamed after our morning in the surf. I continue my exploration, feeling my way over his cheekbones, the hollows of his cheeks, the jut of his chin. "You have beautiful bone structure," I say. That makes him smile, and I realize that's why I said it. I like making him smile.

"Everything about you is beautiful, Rosie."

I shut my eyes, wanting to reject the compliment. I know I'm average. I know he's just being nice. I know that if he really knew me, he wouldn't say that.

"Hey, stop." He puts a finger under my chin. "Whatever you're thinking, you're wrong."

My eyes fly open, then narrow. What does he know? How does he think he knows me after two days? "You're sweet, Gus, but you don't really know me."

"Okay," he says, not offended. "Then let me get to know you better, hermosa." He moves the finger from my chin to the strap of my dress, running it between the fabric and my skin in an unmistakable bid to get me to take it off.

"That's not fair. That's beautiful in Spanish."

"So? From where I'm sitting, eres muy hermosa, chica. It's not really up to you."

His tone is even and light, but he seems prepared to be as stubborn as I can be, so I let this one go. It's not that I want him to think I'm not beautiful. I just don't want him to be disappointed the more he spends time with me.

Then I remember. Three weeks. That's the shelf life of this particular relationship. If he wants to call me beautiful, whatever. We don't have time to be stubborn. I relent and pull my dress up and over my head, leaving me in my swimsuit. It's not like he hadn't spent all morning looking at me in nothing but this, but it's different here, in his bedroom, on an actual bed, actual condoms in my purse.

His eyes gleam and he reaches for one of the straps of the simple tank one piece. He looks at me, a question in his eyes. I nod, and he slips it down, over my shoulder, which causes the front to sag and reveal one of my breasts. He moves as if to kiss me there, but I say, "Wait."

CHAPTER 10

ROSIE

He stops instantly. "What is it, hermosa?"

"Can you?" I indicate his shirt and he takes it off without question. I feel better being mostly naked now that he's caught up, clad only in his board shorts and the spectacular art adorning his chest and back. I feel so much better, actually, that I take one of his hands and place it on my breast. He holds it carefully, palms it as if enjoying the weight of it in his hand. He sweeps his rough thumb over the tip. I gasp.

"Do that again." He repeats the motion obediently, not once, but over and over, relentlessly, until my nipple is peaked and hard. Each pass of his thumb is so intense it's as if he's got his thumb pressed directly to my clit, not just the bud of my nipple.

It's amazing, and I need more. I don't wait for him, just slide the other strap of my suit down, an invitation for him to get to work on the other side. He's been taking his time with me, I can tell, going purposefully slow, but as soon as both breasts are bared, things start moving more quickly.

We kiss again and I find the courage to run my hands up and down the shallow valleys and peaks of Gus's pecs, nipples, abs. He leans into my touch, and I get another rush of that powerful feeling. I have to remind myself that it's been awhile but I have had sex before—good sex. I know what to do, what feels good.

But I've never had sex like this—sex in a brightly lit bedroom during the middle of the day—with someone I'm both desperate to have and just getting to know. There's a push-pull between wanting to rush and taking our time. Gus is treating this like more than a throwaway afternoon delight. He's touching me like something precious, and our being together like this as something to savor.

Where before I was inclined to rush, in order to get it over with and have the nerves of the first time with a new person behind me, now I feel time stretching out before me, endless, with nothing to fill it but Gus's body, and the way it feels against mine.

Soon he replaces his hands with his mouth and if I thought he had a direct line to my clit before, now I'm certain I could come from nothing but his tongue on my tits. I'm so wet, I feel myself soaking through the polyester of my swimsuit. It's suddenly uncomfortable, so I stop him long enough to shimmy all the way out of it.

The breather leads me to a discovery—Gus's erection is making a hell of a tent in his shorts. I feel momentarily awkward that I've neglected his arousal as overcome as I've been with his attention to my body, but it's short-lived, as he simply shucks the shorts off and joins me on the bed. The erection looked impressive when it was trapped under fabric, but freed, it's mouthwatering. He's long and uncut, his penis rising straight up out of thick but neat black pubic hair, a large scrotum to match. He has a vague tan line, the area covered by his shorts a few shades lighter brown than the rest of his skin. He has a mole on his hip that the doctor in me wants to inspect for irregularities, though otherwise he appears to be a perfectly healthy thirty-one-year-old male.

"Hermosa, what are you thinking about?" His fingers dance on my naked hip, drawing me closer.

"I'm thinking about you." This is temporary. We're temporary. It makes me reckless. "I'm thinking that I want to come."

His smile grows wicked. "Any ideas about how you'd like to come?"

I shiver. "Nothing in particular."

"Then let me try something I've wanted to do all day."

"What—" my words turn into a squeak as he pulls me halfway down the bed, my ass nearly to the edge, my legs hanging over the end. He gently presses my thighs apart, dropping to his knees on the floor between them. I rise up onto my elbows, not sure about this turn of events. His eyes are dark as they catch my gaze.

"I need to taste you, hermosa. Can I?"

"Need?" I say breathlessly. That seems like an overstatement. No man has ever enthusiastically gone down on me before. Usually it's a perfunctory checking of the box, so to speak, before requesting oral from me. "Really?"

"Really," he confirms. His gaze drops to my pussy. He doesn't move as he says, "So beautiful. Just as I thought. *Please*, Rosie." He really does sound as if he's suffering and the only relief will come when his mouth licks me into oblivion.

I give in, flopping all the way onto my back. I instinctively spread my legs a little farther open. "Okay, whatever, that's fine." I'm so exposed down there, I throw an arm over my face so I can't see him lowering his mouth to me, but I feel it like an electric shock through my system. His mouth is the defibrillator and he's shocking my heart back online.

After the first jolt, it's just warm, wet pressure, and I relax. Maybe this will be a chill prelude to the main event of vaginal intercourse. Then he flicks the tight bundle of nerves that is my clit with his tongue and I let out an involuntary moan. He alternates between activating that nerve center and licking long, wet stripes along my folds. I'm shaking with arousal, shivering with pleasure. I'm not certain I can take any more of this wizardry, about to beg him to stop, when he sticks his rigid tongue straight into my vagina, spearing into me, while his fingers thrum my clit like a guitar string and I literally explode.

Okay, not literally, but groans pour from my mouth while liquid gushes from my pussy, and pleasure floods my body as every part of me revels in the riot of endorphins and serotonin that is my orgasm. It just goes on and on and on, until when I come back to myself I realize I have Gus's sheets in a death grip and I'm breathing so hard it takes me a while to realize those labored breaths I'm hearing are my own.

Gus presses soft kisses to the inside of my thighs, rises off the floor in a sinuous motion. He's oddly graceful, I notice for the first time. I should have noted it earlier, when we were surfing, where his motions seemed to flow along with the waves, or at the garden, even when he had an injury, he moved through the garden as if he was a part of it and it was a part of him.

Through my post-orgasmic veil I can see his erection hasn't abated in the slightest. If anything, he's harder than before he went down on me. But he doesn't seem concerned about that as he lies down next to me. He doesn't kiss me, but I want to taste myself on him, so I do. He kisses me back enthusiastically. When I wrap my hand around his cock he groans and moves closer, so I tighten my grip.

"That felt…" I want to tell him that I've never come like that from a guy's mouth, but don't know quite how to put it into words. "…incredible."

"I'm glad, beautiful. You taste incredible, too. Petals upon petals. Not to go too far with the flower metaphors."

I laugh. Being named Rosie has its drawbacks, besides the fact that it makes me sound like a seven-year-old.

"I'm not a flower, Gus," I remind him.

"I know. You're a woman," he says, punctuating his words with kisses on my jaw. "More beautiful than any flower in any garden."

"Stop, seriously."

"I am serious."

I glare at him, but he's perfectly calm. "I know flowers. I know how pollination works, too, and I'm not ready for that, so are you on birth control?"

"Wow. Um, yes." I'm impressed with how calmly he brought it up. "I have an IUD. I have condoms in my bag, too."

"I've got some, hermosa, unless you want to use yours."

"Yours are fine."

"Okay."

Neither of us moves. What is he waiting for? It hits me— he's let me lead this entire time. He's asked for what he wants, but he's also never done anything without my permission.

"I want you inside me," I say, feeling slightly ridiculous, but so, so turned on.

He groans, kisses me, and rolls over to get a condom from his bedside drawer. Then he lies back so I can watch him roll on the condom.

"Come on, hermosa," he says, pulling me on top of him. How does he know that I love this position? I climb over him quickly, straddling his thighs, and I rub my drenched pussy along the sheathed length of his cock. The hard ridge feels so good that my legs are already shaking when I tilt my hips, catching his erection on the mouth of my pussy.

The slide down as I take him inside me seems to last forever, until finally I'm flush with him, joined as intimately as possible. I take a moment to adjust to the feeling of being filled, appreciating anew that he's not in rush to get to the main event. I've been with guys who seem to view sex as glorified jerking off, just a race to see who comes first. It's never a surprise who wins that particular race. But Gus seems to be enjoying every aspect of this, in no hurry to see it end.

I like the way his hands grip my waist, gentle but sure, and I put my hands on his chest for leverage as I experiment with sliding up and down a few inches. God, it's good, but a lot. Even as wet as I am, I feel stretched and I'm not sure if this is going to work.

"Rosie? Okay?"

"I'm just—yeah—" I must make a face or something, because he's quick to respond.

"Hang on." He shifts, does something with the angle of his hips, and then suddenly everything gets easier. The pressure feels good, not uncomfortable, and we start moving together, his abs flexing as he does most of the heavy lifting, so to speak, while I control things from my end with rolling hips and clenching thighs. I might feel some underused muscles tomorrow. I hope I do.

"Better?" he asks.

"Better."

"Let's see if we can do better than better," he says, and picks up the pace.

I let out a yelp as the angle and the pace makes my clit bounce hard against his pelvis with every thrust, each time sending stars spinning through my body. "Yes, that's, that's much better," I manage, and he half-smiles, but he's too intent on the business at hand to complete the expression. We might have been playing before. Now it's serious. He's on a mission to make this good for me, and he's not going to let anything stop him. I'm not about to complain, since I feel my second orgasm of the day bearing down.

"Don't stop." If I had the presence of mind to analyze my voice, it might sound like I'm begging. I don't care. "Please."

"I won't stop, hermosa," he grits out.

I'm bouncing in time to his thrusts, my entire body taut,

except for my breasts, which are jiggling up and down, but since Gus's gaze is pretty much glued to them, I don't feel self-conscious in the least. I feel sexy. I feel appreciated.

"I'm coming," I gasp, even though Gus can probably tell. His grip on me tightens, his eyes close, and he's shouting through his own release. The lightness of the room means I can see him perfectly clearly as he cascades with pleasure.

I never thought men in the throes of orgasm were particularly attractive—it's so animalistic and raw, their faces screwed up in effort, red and sweaty and, for a moment, helpless. But on Gus, an orgasm looks almost beautiful. His mouth is an O, his long black lashes lay against his face, his back is arched, exposing the line of his beautifully inked torso. I drink in the sheer masculine gracefulness that he exhibits even in the most basic of human physical experiences.

I come back to myself slowly. I'm hot and sticky. My hair is twice as tangled as before. Gus runs his hands up my sides, as if he doesn't want to stop touching me. I lean over, fit my mouth over his. He kisses me eagerly. It feels good to do it, like it was something we missed while we were doing the other stuff.

Eventually, we disengage, and he finds some tissues and disposes of the condom. I'm suddenly tired, between the surfing and the sex. I yawn loudly, then clap a hand over my mouth in embarrassment. "Sorry."

"No worries, hermosa. Rest."

He lies back down, pulls me into a loose embrace. I smell him, earthy and salty. He smells like he tastes, and I shiver a little at the knowledge. Everything about this day has been so unlike me, and consequently felt so good, that tears prick my eyes.

"Thank you." I whisper to avoid sounding like I'm going to cry, because crying after sex is absolutely the most annoying girl thing to do.

There's a smile in Gus's voice. "Rosie, you don't have to thank me, seriously."

"I know." But I do. I feel a wash of gratitude that I met him, that I had the courage to ask him for this. That he found me worthy of giving it to me. He rubs his cheek against my hair. His sheets smell like us. His bed is comfortable.

I blink away the single tear that escapes, and then blink a couple of times more, and then I'm asleep.

CHAPTER 11
GUS

After Rosie falls asleep, I guess I do, too, because when I open my eyes again, the room is dim. Rosie's on the right side of my bed taking up the real estate like it's got her name on it. She looks softer in sleep, the lines of her usually take-charge face smoothed away. Her hair, so severely pulled back the day I met her, is a tangled cloud. My heart does a weird little flip when I think how in control she likes to be and how comfortable she must be to let go enough with me to be that serene.

I stretch my arms, trying not to jostle her. My body feels good—worn out in a different way than I usually feel after a long day of physical activity. Until we got back to my place, I wasn't sure Rosie would really go through with it—but damn, I'm glad she did.

Her body is ripe, wet and sweet and soft, and we fit together. Sure, it took a little adjustment—first-time sex isn't always a home run—but feeling the way she came apart under my mouth, riding on top of me, it was definitely worth it.

I want to let her sleep a little longer, so I get up quietly, use the bathroom, and put on a fresh pair of shorts. Rosie seems to like me without a shirt, so I don't bother with one. I'm trying to decide what we should do for dinner—eat out or in?—when the girl in my bed rolls over and opens her eyes.

"Hey," she says, her voice thick with sleep.

"Hey." I hope this isn't the only chance I get to see her wake up, because it's truly an experience. She's still naked, so I get a full view of her gorgeous breasts when she stretches out like a cat, and then I get an equally stunning view of her ass when she gets out of bed to go to the bathroom. I'm glad I thought to clean up a little while I was in there before. Girls don't like most single guys' idea of acceptable bathroom cleanliness levels.

She pokes her head out of the doorway to ask if she can take a shower.

"Of course. I'll get you a towel."

"Thanks." Her smile is shy, which is both cute and worrying. Does this mean that it's over, this "fling," after one round of great sex? I normally don't care whether a girl wants to stick around or not—I'm content with what I have, and yeah, regular sex is a nice perk of having a girlfriend, but it so often comes with pressure and expectations. But that's something that Rosie seems to be as averse to as me.

And if she thinks that what we did this afternoon is the best I've got, she's dead wrong. I have to show her that our fling is far from over.

She's not long in the shower, but I manage to make the bed and bring her a glass of water from the kitchen. She drinks it thirstily, the towel I handed her through the door wrapped around her tightly.

Her hair is wet, her face scrubbed clean. Her lips are naturally pink, like a Knockout rose, but I keep that observation to myself. She probably thinks all of my flower allusions are lame or calculated. Hey, I won't deny that I've used my botanical knowledge to sweet-talk females in the past.

Is this different? On a primal level, I don't want it to be. I'm not sure I'm prepared for this to be different. But on another level, the level where I can't lie to myself, I know it is.

Roses are ubiquitous for a reason. They're always beautiful, no matter if they're tightly held buds or peak blooms or fading and carelessly dropping petals. They're also dangerous. They make you work for it, pricking without mercy, without judgment—unless you're careful. Do I need to be careful with Rosie?

"I can't believe I fell asleep," she says, setting the water glass down on the night table. She doesn't immediately go for her clothes, which is promising.

"I fell asleep, too. I can't remember the last time I took a nap."

"Sometimes I do if I'm on call at the hospital and I end up working a long shift."

"You hungry? I was thinking pizza."

"Oh." She looks surprised.

"Didn't you say you'd have dinner with me?"

"Yeah, but...never mind."

"What? You thought I'd kick you out after sleeping with you?"

"No!"

I can tell the thought did cross her mind. I fold my arms over my chest.

"Listen, Rosie. I know we're doing things a little out of order here. This is some kind of vacation-type thing for you, and that's fine. We don't know each other that well, but I'm not an asshole. I promise." It grates that she'd think I'd ditch her the moment I got in her pants.

"I didn't think you were," she says quickly. "I apologize if I gave that impression."

She's so beautiful standing in my bedroom, her hair damp, in nothing but my best bath towel. Now that I've seen her naked, I find myself wanting that state to be the default. She's really, really sexy. Not sexy like the girls who paint their faces and lacquer their nails and wear spiky heels and ass-hugging skirts, which, don't get me wrong, I appreciate as much as the next guy. But Rosie's...unvarnished. She's raw. Delicate. Soft skin, succulent pussy. My mouth waters when I remember how she tasted, just as salty-sweet as I knew she would.

I cross over to her, take one of her hands in mine. "I like you," I say, kissing my way across her knuckles softly. "And your vacation isn't over. So this isn't either."

"Okay." I barely hear her, she's whispering so softly. "That sounds good."

"Because I thought that before was pretty awesome, but we can do better."

"Can we?" She lets out a flustered laugh as I loosen the towel enough to slip my hand underneath and caress her ribs, pulling her close to me.

"The second time is always better than the first."

"Really?" She looks doubtful. "The best head of my life is going to be hard to top."

The compliment turns me rock hard in seconds. "Just give me a chance." I kiss a line from her jaw to her collarbone, working my way further under the towel, until it pools around our feet and her breasts are pressed against my chest.

She shudders as my kisses trail lower, skimming the top of her breasts, then pay lavish attention to each nipple in turn. Her breasts are full underneath and sloped on top, the tips pointed and perfect.

Now that I've mapped her folds and ridges with my tongue, I feel them with my fingers, keeping my touch light, almost teasing, until she gets fed up and starts pressing her mound into my palm, seeking more friction. I give it to her, letting her grind against my hand, then against my hip, as I fumble to release the buttons and zipper on my shorts. We stumble back against the bed and I hope I haven't oversold my prowess. She's got me so hard, so needy, despite having come once today so hard I practically blacked out, I feel like I won't last.

But maybe it's not about showing off or showing her that we're in for three weeks of incredible sex. Maybe it's just about what feels good right now, because I have to have her and she's just as desperate. When we're lying down and I touch her pussy again, this time it's swollen and wet, and I know it's going to feel so good to get my cock inside her again.

"Hermosa," I sigh raggedly, when she closes her fist around me and guides me to her wet entrance, "condom."

"Oh shit," she says, and lets go.

I leave her just long enough to get one. She's nestled against my sheets like she belongs there. I struggle to remember a time before she was in my bed, and I can't. I don't want to. Instead, I roll on the condom and her eyes watch my progress hungrily. I touch her breasts. "Will you hold these for me, hermosa?" They're so sensitive, and I want to see her bringing herself pleasure.

Her eyes widen a little, then she cups herself, softly at first, then a little harder once I settle back between her legs. "That's right," I say. "Do whatever feels good. You're so beautiful like that."

I slide into her, and I wasn't wrong. It feels better than the first time. Will every time be like this, better than the last? Will we ever reach a point when it won't feel like heaven to slide into her warm, slick pussy?

"You feel so good," I say, in a major understatement. I lean down, and we fit together well enough that I can kiss her in this position, tasting her cherry lips, chasing her flavor with my tongue, trying to place it. Is it the spice from the salsa at breakfast or is it the way my soap smells on her skin? I kiss and kiss her, her breasts trapped between us, my cock buried as deep as it will go.

She's panting when we pull apart. "Fuck me. Please."

I groan and immediately pull out only to slam back in again. It's too good, she's too hot, too soft, too wet, for me to last longer than a few pathetic strokes, but I grit my teeth and hang on. She moans in time with my thrusts, her fingers tightening over the flesh of her tits, the flesh spilling between her fingers. She takes her thumb and forefinger and pinches her nipples tight and then she lets out a sound, low and long, and her eyes fly open.

"Fuck, I'm coming," she says, confirming my suspicion. I don't stop, letting her ride it out, and then when I can't hold off any longer, I put my weight on one arm so I can find her clit with my other hand, pressing down as I spill into her, dimly hearing her panting, moaning, maybe even screaming. I love it that she's not holding back, that she's taking as good as she's giving, that she's not letting her natural shyness get in the way of experiencing this.

Because that's what I figured about Rosie from the very beginning. She might be a confident, badass doctor, but she's shy. Reserved with those she doesn't know well. I feel privileged to be someone she can relax and be herself with. If she's not yet, I vow that she will be.

We come down together, sweaty and rumpled again. My sheets haven't seen this much action in a while, and it pains me to think I'll have to wash the smell of woman off of them eventually.

"So the second time's always better, huh?" she says from the spot in the crook of my arm where she fits perfectly. "Is that your theory?"

"It's very scientific," I say.

"I'm sure you have a broad sample size," she says.

"Not as big as you might think," I say. I'm not a player, and it's suddenly important that she know that.

"Like, approximately how big, would you say?"

Okay, she wants to do this. I do a quick count in my head. "Um, approximately a dozen, off the top of my head."

"Okay. That seems like a decent sample." She doesn't sound upset or relieved, just neutral.

"What about you?" I don't really care, but maybe she brought it up because she wants me to know.

"Somewhat smaller sample size," she says, keeping up our jokey shield. "Um, six? You're seven."

"Lucky number seven."

She laughs. "I guess so."

"Well, hermosa, you're the best second time I've ever had."

"Really?"

"Really."

When she next speaks, her voice is tentative. "I've never come easily in that position."

I feel a stab of guilt. I should have tried something else, made sure she was enjoying it, even though all signs pointed to yes. "Missionary isn't your thing, noted."

"But that was, I don't know, it felt really good. Touching myself. When you touched me. I liked it. A lot."

I'm so relieved, I can't hold back from curling over to kiss her. Somehow, in the short span of a day, this woman's pleasure has become priority one for me. I want to make her feel the best she's ever felt. I want to take care of her. She doesn't seem to have anyone whose job it is to spoil her, to put her first. It's a job I didn't apply for, but now that I'm in the running, I'm determined to land it.

CHAPTER 12

ROSIE

Gus orders pizza while I shower again, briefly, and get dressed in the change of clothes I brought—jeans and a blue T-shirt. I hope the pizza gets here fast; I'm ravenous after having missed lunch and then having sex—twice. I can't remember the last time I had sex twice in one day. Honestly, that particular miracle may never have happened before.

My previous relationships occurred in two distinct eras—college and med school. College dating consisted of tentative kisses with painfully awkward fellow pre-meds, and one honest-to-God boyfriend who lasted a few months before we mutually decided we just weren't into each other. Med school and residency were more about hookups and booty calls. We'd battle egos and our instructors during the day and then take out our frustrations on each other after hours.

I never met anyone who distracted me from my ultimate goal of becoming a doctor, and none of the guys I hooked up with seemed to want more from me, so it all worked out. It got lonely, of course. But loneliness has been my baseline since I was thirteen. The lack of a serious relationship in my life didn't —doesn't—bother me.

While we wait for dinner, I make good on my promise to check Gus's hand. It's healing quickly, but I dab on some antibacterial ointment to be on the safe side. Gus shows me the patio table and chairs on the concrete apron outside his bedroom door. I sip on the root beer he brings me while he sets out plates, napkins, a huge bowl of chips, and a smaller one of hummus.

"So domestic," I say, digging into the chips and hummus shamelessly.

"Just 'cause I'm a single guy doesn't mean I don't know how to live."

"Clearly." I may be a little defensive, considering if Gus saw the inside of my refrigerator right now he'd be blinded by the reflection of light off empty shelves. "How are you still single, then?"

Gus laughs, startled. "Shit. Well, you know how it is."

"Not really."

"I'm not much of a planner. Most of the girls I've dated don't like it when I don't want to talk about the future. I sort of like to let things go a day at a time."

"Really?" I'm surprised. Gus may be miles more spontaneous than I am—what else would you call his invitation to me the day we first encountered each other? But he's put down roots, literally, whereas I've been in the same place for two years and I've barely carved out enough space in my own life for...a life.

Then again, what does it matter that Gus doesn't do long term? That's perfect for this whole three-week affair we've embarked on. I should be glad he's not involved with anyone else and won't get all weird when we reach our expiration date.

"Then I guess I picked the right person for my staycation fling." I try for a sophisticated and worldly expression and ruin the effect by taking a sip of my caffeine-free root beer. I sigh. I might as well be drinking from a juice box.

Gus gives me a slightly confused smile, then jumps up to grab the pizza when a knock comes on the door.

Night falls as we consume the entire delicious pizza, along with plenty of beer, regular and root, and all of the chips and hummus. The sounds of the neighborhood provide a soothing backdrop to our conversation, which is mainly about harmless things like favorite pizza toppings and places to eat in Ventura. A dog barks, some little kids bike down the street yelling, a baby cries. It's soothing and a far cry from the sounds I hear from my condo, which is usually nothing.

"How's it feel so far? Your staycation?" Gus asks, stretching his legs out in front of him. He produces a toothpick from somewhere and chews on it absently.

"To be honest? Weird. I keep thinking they're going to call me back into the hospital."

"You love what you do, don't you?"

"Being a doctor? Yeah. I really love it."

"Why?"

"Why?" The question stumps me. "I—it's all I ever wanted to be."

"Wow. That's so cool."

"You didn't know you wanted to work in a garden when you were a kid?"

He laughs. "I didn't know it was even a job. If you told me I'd be a gardener when I was a grownup, I would have pictured walking around with a leaf blower all day. No. I didn't know what I was going to be, but not that."

"Then how did you get into it?"

Instead of answering, he gets up and walks to a makeshift table made out of plywood and sawhorses. It's covered in small pots, some plastic, some terra-cotta. Most of them hold plants of one kind or another. He picks up a few and pulls off a few brown leaves as he talks.

"I wasn't a very good student. It wasn't because I couldn't do the work. It was more that I thought being inside all day was a form of cruel and unusual punishment. Homework was torture. I wanted to be outside, playing with my friends. I was obsessed with skateboarding, took the bus to the beach to surf when I should have been in school, stuff like that."

I get a picture in my mind of young Gus getting up before dawn to go surfing instead of school, and smile.

"I like to *do* things, be active. It's okay if my brain gets involved, too. I like to read, if it's about something that interests me. But school was tough. My parents are second-generation, met in college, have solid careers. It was important to them that my sister and I go to college, that we rise up the ladder even further than they did." He sighs, as if reliving years of parental disapproval.

"I had this—this is embarrassing now—I had this stupid dream that I could be a professional skateboarder, maybe get into the X Games scene. Of course, that was completely unthinkable to Mom and Dad. We fought all the time, until I finally moved out. I was at loose ends, bumming around, half-heartedly going to community college. I almost signed up for the Army, just to get away and start over."

I try to imagine Gus in the Army and get stuck on how cute he'd look in uniform. I put that thought on hold as he goes on.

"One day I was riding my skateboard down Main Street and there was this older guy doing the strangest thing." He stops, returns to his seat next to me, takes a sip of beer.

"What was he doing?" I'm hooked on Gus's story, wondering how a kid who had to repeat World History in high school ended up tending a palm tree forest and making his own hybrids in his backyard.

"He was reaching into the amaryllis in the planters on Main Street, then putting his hand in his pockets. Like, real quick." He demonstrates the gesture for me; it does look odd.

"Why?"

"I followed him for a while, trying to figure out what he was doing. Finally, I rode up to him and asked him what was up. He looked around, and whispered, 'Collecting seeds.' He was harvesting seeds from the plants and was going to take them home to propagate them."

"Is that illegal?"

"Let's just say it's frowned upon, especially in a garden like Pacifica Park."

"So why the sketchiness?"

"He started telling me he'd collected seeds from all over the world and he'd learned to be real subtle about it. I was fascinated. I had never heard of someone dealing in plants, at least for something other than pot."

I laugh. There was plenty of that kind of thing where we grew up.

"He told me he had a backyard nursery where he propagated unusual species and then sold them to nurseries and gardens. He needed an assistant, someone to water when he was out of town, to lift and carry heavy stuff. I followed him home that afternoon. I was shocked when I saw his so-called backyard nursery. You think this is impressive?" He points at his collection. "He probably had a hundred-thousands dollars' worth of plants right in his backyard. No wonder he kept things on the down low—if people in the right circles knew about it, he'd be robbed."

"Do people actually do that? Steal plants?"

"All the time. Bring a shovel, go to a park in the middle of the night, dig up a twenty-foot palm, sell it for a few grand. Little risk and high margins."

"Whoa." Plant theft? Who knew?

"I couldn't believe this was his life, not just his job. He got to be outside, among beautiful plants, all day long, every day. He made good money at it. I thought, I'm not going to be a pro skateboarder or in the X Games, and I'm sure as hell not going to be a teacher or an accountant or whatever else my parents want me to be. But this was something I could see myself doing, see myself *being*."

He nudges my calf with his toe. I've been staring off into the back yard, but now I turn and meet his gaze. He looks at me like he knows me. I wish all there was for him to know was the boring workaholic girl he took pity on and ended up in bed with.

"Because what we do is who we are, isn't it, Rosie?"

I've equated what I do with who I am for so long, I'm having an identity crisis not being able to do that thing for three lousy days.

Deflection is second nature. "So you learned from him. What was his name?"

"Naoki Sasamoto. I guess I became his apprentice. He taught me everything from the ground up—no pun intended."

I arch a single eyebrow, one of my few natural talents.

"Okay, pun a little bit intended."

"That's what I thought."

"He taught me about soil, water, sun. He taught me the scientific names of the plants. Eventually, he showed me how to germinate, hybridize, graft. His specialty was palms, so that's where I started, but I learned about everything. Eventually, he had to pull back on work, and that's when I got the job at Pacifica Park. He knew my boss, Flora, got me an interview. I've been there..." he pauses to count back "...six years now."

"Amazing."

"Naoki was amazing." His expression turns sad for a second. I've seen Gus look mischievous, happy, even orgasmic, but this is the first time I've seen him look sad. "He died last year."

"I'm sorry." I know from experience that saying anything more won't help, so I leave it at that.

"Thanks."

We sit in silence for a while. The night brings out the sweetness in the air. Sweet—that's how it feels to sit with Gus in the calm oasis of his own private garden.

I feel the pull to go back inside, into the cocoon of warmth and pleasure that I'd find in Gus's bed. But getting back in his bed means spending the night, and it's dangerous to set that precedent. You aren't supposed to cuddle and sleep and share intimacies with your vacation fling, and we've already kind of done that, if the between-orgasms nap we had counts.

I make a quick pro and con list in my head.

Pro: if I spend the night, then we'll end up having sex again.

Con: if I spend the night, we'll end up having breakfast together. We'll end up kissing and talking and our lives will cease to be about a friendly, convenient, mutually satisfying, sex-based temporary relationship, and will veer toward something...else. Something I can't afford and don't want. Something I won't have time for in three weeks anyway.

"Gus?" I say his name like a question and feel dumb. It's just the two of us here.

"Yes, Rosie?" he says, infinitely patient. He's let me set the pace the entire time. I'm grateful, but I don't know how to say that.

"Thanks for taking me surfing, and for breakfast, and the other things."

"The other things?"

"You know. The sex." Why is it embarrassing to verbalize it, when I wasn't embarrassed the two times he was inside me?

"Oh that." He shrugs. "Anytime."

I smile. I know he's playing it cool. I'm starting to get that his casual tone doesn't mean things don't matter to him.

"I'll take you surfing anytime, hermosa. Breakfast, too. How about tomorrow?"

I bite my lip. I know what he's really asking. "I think I better go home. I have a wedding planning meeting with Nicole and the other bridesmaids tomorrow."

"Okay." He doesn't seem disappointed, and he doesn't try to change my mind. I've never met a guy so content to let me lead.

We take the detritus of our dinner back into the house. I find my bag, locate my shoes under Gus's bed. It feels strange to slide sandals onto my feet after having been barefoot most of the day. For once I've been able to enjoy the sight of my pink-painted toenails, usually hidden under my sensible work shoes. Today I've touched the sand, swum in the ocean, had multiple orgasms in someone else's bed, gotten clean in someone else's shower. It's not me, but it's been a relief to pretend to be someone else for a while.

Gus gives me a lingering kiss before I go. He's a good enough kisser that I'm questioning all of my life choices as I say, "See you soon," instead of pulling him back to the bedroom.

"I hope so," he says. I know he means it.

I can't help wondering "Why?" on my drive home. Why didn't I stay? Why didn't he try harder to get me to? Why do I care? Why is he spending so much time with me anyway? I must be taking him away from his friends, his family. I don't know the answers to these questions, but I have an inkling of trepidation that I'm even thinking about this stuff at all. In the past, I've never had an issue giving up a sexual partner when it started interfering with my work. I try to reassure myself that this time isn't any different at all.

The leap my pulse takes when I slide into my parking spot behind my condo and notice I have a text belies my nonchalance. Instead of something charming or sweet from Gus, the text is from my brother, Jake.

JAKE SNYDER

Mom's anniversary is coming up. Meet at the usual place? Or do you have to work?

All the buzz from my wonderful day with Gus drains out of me in an instant. How could I have forgotten?

No, I didn't forget. I've just been busy with something besides punishing myself for a change. A knot of guilt and sadness forms in my stomach, getting bigger the longer I stare at the message. I text back, typing the words out slowly.

> I'm not working. I'll be there. Friday? 10 AM?

He replies almost instantly.

> OK, good. I'll bring the flowers.

I think for a second, then type out another text.

> How are you?

I wait in my car for a few more minutes, but no reply comes. Eventually, I get out and let myself into my dark condo, foregoing a shower to slip under my ratty old quilt, sadness tingeing my mood. The feeling is as comfortable as the quilt, and just as familiar. It reminds me who I am. I'm not the fun, carefree girl who goes surfing and has sex with hot plant whisperers, who eats pizza with her bare feet tucked up underneath her. No, I'm Dr. Rosie Snyder, workaholic orphan and terrible sister. I fall asleep feeling alone as ever.

CHAPTER 13

ROSIE

When I roll out of bed, the twinge of muscles I haven't used in years brings yesterday's adventures flooding back to me in a rush. Sand and salt water. Huevos rancheros and pizza. Gus's mouth. Gus's hands. Gus's strong chest, his thick... Shit, I have to get ready for brunch.

I move through some yoga poses, admittedly impatiently, but it's good to stretch, to feel the burn of my thighs, the tenderness of my arms. The pull and tug of my body reminds me I'm alive. Even if I barely recognize my life at the moment, at least I'm living.

I check my phone. There's only a single text from Nicole. Nothing from Gus. Nothing from Jake. Radio silence from my brother is normal, so I put him out of my mind. If I haven't heard from Gus by the afternoon, I can text him myself if I want to. In the meantime, I prepare for the bridesmaid brunch as if I'm going to battle.

I dress with care, in a twin to yesterday's sundress, this one black with small white flowers embroidered around the edges. I take more time with my makeup than usual, knowing at least

Nicole and Lani will appreciate the effort. If I end up seeing Gus later, well, then I won't mind looking my best.

When I walk into the dining room of one of the swankiest hotels in Santa Barbara later that morning, I'm glad I've made an effort. This is supposed to be an informal wedding planning session with Nicole and the four bridesmaids, but leave it to Nicole to choose the oldest of old-money locales for the occasion. The flower-bedecked room is beautiful, inviting, and expensive. Just like Nicole.

"You're here!" Nicole exclaims as if we haven't seen each other in years, even though we only just spent the day together. Lani, Nicole's business partner, waves from the opposite side of the table. I've only met her once, and I'm woman enough to admit I'm intimidated by her dry, cutting sense of humor—and her clothes. She's wearing a one-piece jumpsuit in a complicated floral pattern, mustard yellow ankle boots, and heavy gold jewelry at her neck and ears. She's not conventionally gorgeous, but she's got style for days.

Nicole wraps me in a boa-constrictor-like hug, and only lets go when I grunt. When I get my breath back I say, "Hi, Ophelia. Hi, Kate."

Ophelia waves slightly. If I didn't already know she's a school librarian, it would have been my first guess. Her long dark-blonde hair is held in a bun at the back of her head, while her high-necked pink blouse shows off her pale complexion but manages to hide her figure and make her look about twelve.

If Ophelia is quiet and Lani cool as a cucumber, Kate is warm like a sunny late-summer morning. She stands up and hugs me slightly less enthusiastically than Nicole, for which I am grateful. She pushes her long red hair behind her ears and grins. "Thank God you're here. I think Nicole might have an aneurysm if she has to wait any longer before pulling out the bridal magazines."

"Not much you can do for an aneurysm," I say. There's a short pause before Kate laughs, a loud chuckle that echoes off the walls of the dining room. A few gray-haired ladies turn to look.

Besides Nicole, I've known Kate the longest. She went to UCLA with us, and even though her major was theater we had a few classes together, which is why I know her the best of the bunch. I've always liked her no-nonsense personality, but I was so busy with my class load I didn't socialize as much as she and Nicole. Actually, in college no one socialized as much as Nicole.

I've only seen Kate a handful of times since—well, since the accident—but she doesn't seem much different than the energetic, sardonic teenager I used to know. She's dressed even more casually than me, in jeans and a T-shirt that hangs loosely off one shoulder, exposing a bright blue lace bra strap. I wonder what the gray-hairs think of that as I take my seat at the round table.

Nicole sits, the picture window framing her against the competing blues of the Pacific Ocean and the sky. I'm witnessing a queen taking her throne while her dutiful handmaidens await her proclamations.

She's blonder than her cousin, salon-induced waves of hair undulating down the sides of her face, terminating artfully at the top of her generous breasts. She's perfectly turned out in a sheath dress and flats, more debutante than bride, but old habits die hard.

"Before we start hammering out the details of this massive undertaking, I just want to say again how very, very grateful I am that you all agreed to take this journey with me." It doesn't sound rehearsed, but it probably was.

"Hey, you aren't marrying *us*," Kate reminds her.

"True, but I've known you all, except Lani, longer than I've known Ricky. You ladies know me better than anyone, and you know how ecstatic I am that this is happening, but I just cannot do it without you. So thank you."

I exchange glances with the other girls. We're all fond of Nicole, but she might be taking this sisterhood thing a little far. I barely know Ophelia and Lani. Not to mention that Nicole and Ricky have been together since college—theirs is not exactly a whirlwind romance. They've been a couple for almost a decade and have lived together almost the entire time. I'm not a hundred percent sure why they waited so long to get engaged, but once the ring officially slid onto her finger, Nicole became a different person—not just wedding-obsessed, but obsessed with making her wedding the wedding to end all weddings.

"We're all so happy for you," Ophelia murmurs, since Nicole has paused expectantly.

"I've taken the liberty of adding you all to a Slack channel where we can exchange ideas, pictures, and info as this thing shapes up. And don't freak out, but I need your sizes ASAP so we can start ordering the moment we find the perfect dresses."

I don't know why anybody would freak out. Lani's whip thin, Ophelia's curvy but petite. Kate's the most robust of us all, which means she has a fabulous rack and a tiny waist. All in all, we're a fine bunch of California girls. If I didn't know how intimately each of us is connected to Nicole, I might suspect that she chose us solely for our aesthetic appeal. She's probably imagined herself standing at the alter—a queen surrounded by her ladies in waiting, each one lovelier than the last. But none as lovely as the queen herself, of course.

"Are you doing this thing in a church?" I ask.

"Venue! One of the most important pieces of the puzzle." Nicole grabs one of the Santa Barbara-centric bridal magazines from the table and flips to a page that has been tagged with a neon green sticky note. With that, we wade into the wedding planning weeds.

* * *

A mushroom omelet, two cups of coffee, and ten bridal magazines later, I'm thoroughly sick of offering opinions on various shades of lavender and whether or not the zoo is too "out there" for a wedding destination. I want to be supportive, but the truth is, I don't really care about any of this stuff. I want her to tell me which dress to buy, where to show up, and I'll happily stand with her as she marries Ricky. Otherwise, wedding planning is definitely not my bag.

My thoughts are easily distracted, and the topic they mostly stray to is Gus. I wonder what he's doing with this beautiful Sunday and imagining he might be spending it with someone else. Thinking about Gus reminds me how tired I am after a bad night of sleep, confusion over not staying the night at his place keeping me tossing and turning.

"We're losing Rosie," Nicole says cheerfully as I relax back into my chair and close my eyes, just for a second.

"I'm awake. Just resting my eyes." I perfected the art of the sleepless nap in med school.

"Maybe we could talk about something besides the wedding for a minute," Lani says.

There's a moment of silence as we all digest that sacrilegious suggestion.

"Okay, fine. Rosie, tell us about the party you went to on Friday," Nicole says.

My eyes spring open to meet Nicole's inquisitive gaze. The relief in the other three women at getting a reprieve from wedding talk is tangible.

"It was fun."

"Come on, I need details. What about that guy who asked you? Gus? Isn't that the name of one of the mice from Cinderella?" If there's one thing that Nicole would rather talk about than her own wedding, it's other people's love lives.

"He's nice. And Gus is short for Gustavo." I should have been prepared for this, but it hadn't once occurred to me to figure out how much to tell Nicole and the others about my spontaneous staycation fling. This is what I get for not having many close girlfriends. I'm totally inept at girl talk—especially when it comes to talking about boys.

"Nice? Sounds like a dud," Lani says succinctly.

"Ignore her, Rosie. Some girls actually like nice boys," Nicole scolds. "Are you going to see him again? Since you have time to fill anyway."

"What does that mean?" Kate asks.

"This is so embarrassing. I kind of didn't take any PTO for two years, so the hospital is forcing me to take three weeks off."

"You aren't working for three weeks?" Ophelia says. "Sounds amazing. I would get so much reading done."

"It's growing on me," I admit.

"And what about Gus?" Nicole can tell I'm holding back. "Is *he* going to be keeping you company during your staycation?"

"He still has to work, you know. But we'll probably be seeing each other." It doesn't feel right to reveal we already slept together. Not that I'm ashamed, but I don't want to give Nicole any more ammunition for her little matchmaking heart.

"Maybe the two of you will be next!"

I scrunch my face up in confusion. "Next?"

"The next to get married."

"Here we go," Lani says, leaning forward in her chair as if preparing to watch a boxing match.

My palms start to itch as Nicole continues on the theme. "Ladies, it's incredible to be in a committed relationship. So much stability, so much security."

"So much boredom," Lani says under her breath.

Nicole totally hears her and shoots her a look. "I want the four of you to really think about this. We're thirty now—except for O, who's still a baby. We're not getting any younger."

"I'm telling my mom you're infringing on her intellectual property. She gave me this speech last week," Lani says.

Nicole ignores her. "When I think of how happy I am to wake up next to Ricky every day and know that I'm going to get to do that every day for the rest of my life—it's just *bliss*."

Nicole truly looks blissed out, as if her monogamous relationship has brought her to some altered state where she hovers above us mere mortals and pronounces upon us what's wrong with our lives.

"Not that I think you have to have a man to be happy"— Nicole pauses so we can all mentally insert *of course you do*— "but it makes my heart hurt to think that while I've found true love, you're still wandering around in singledom. It's such a waste. You gals are such catches.

"Once this wedding is over, I'm making it my mission to see that each and every one of you is as happy as I am."

With that, she rises from the table, tosses her hair, and announces, "I'm going to pee."

"Well that was ominous," Ophelia says darkly once Nicole has gone. "Do you think she fancies herself a matchmaker?"

"God, I hope not," Lani says. "She has terrible taste in men, no offense to Ricky."

I laugh. Ricky is nice, but a little vanilla. I've never seen him in anything less formal than a Lacoste shirt and boat shoes. He's handsome, in a generic way, and while he's obviously devoted to Nicole, he offers none of the same dramatic creative energy that she does.

"I'll tell the three of you right now: I'm never getting married. Nicole can match-make until she's blue in the face. It's not happening." Kate's determination is evident in her flat tone. Considering she's come the closest of any of us to tying the knot, I can't blame her.

"Me either," Lani agrees with a surprising vehemence. "I'm happy for Nicole. But marriage—so *not* for everyone." She glances out the window at the ocean view. "Definitely not for me." I wonder what—or who—she's thinking about.

"That makes three of us," Ophelia puts in. "I'm never getting married either."

At twenty-five maybe Ophelia's too young to make that statement with such confidence, but I remember how focused on med school I was at that age. A relationship was the last thing on my to-do list. She's old enough to know her own mind.

"Nicole thinks I just need to meet the right guy. But that's not it. I like being single. Some things are more important than relationships." Ophelia doesn't sound bitter, just firm. My respect for her grows the longer we hang out, especially because she's the closest thing Nicole has to a sister, and none of Nicole's frankly retro relationship views seem to have rubbed off on her. She must be one strong lady.

"What about you?" Kate asks, turning to me. "Are you looking for Mr. Right?"

I shrug. "Marriage has never been in my plans." It's the truth. The main reason for getting married is to have kids, and I'm not having kids.

Still, my answer is a bit disingenuous. I haven't dated in a long time, but the last couple of days with Gus have been more than nice. Maybe I've underestimated the health benefits of regular sex. It's good for you, like spinning or cauliflower rice. Even if I can't make room for a more committed relationship, I fleetingly wonder how Gus would feel about our fling turning into a friends-with-benefits situation when our three weeks is up.

Casual sex is one thing and marriage is something else entirely. Nicole really is delusional if she thinks matrimony is the magic bullet that will solve anyone in this room's problems. I let out a short laugh. "Poor Nicole, she's going to be so disappointed if she doesn't get to be a bridesmaid because the four of us never get married."

"She'll get used to the disappointment," Ophelia says.

"Still, we better not rub her face in it until after the wedding," Kate says. "She's so happy right now."

"Fair," Lani says. "But if she keeps up with this matchmaking stuff, we have to stick together. Strength in numbers—four of us and one of her. We gotta be tough. No one can make us get married if we don't want to." She stares at each one of us in turn with her intensely dark eyes.

"Agreed," I say, and the other two nod solemnly, as if we've reached a pact.

"What's agreed?" Nicole's back, an intrigued expression on her face.

"Oh, nothing you need to concern yourself with," Lani says airily. "Just bridesmaid stuff."

Nicole puts a hand on her hip and grins. "Are you planning the bachelorette party already? You guys! I'll send you some ideas I had later. It's going to be epic!"

CHAPTER 14

ROSIE

I t's mid-afternoon by the time we say our goodbyes. When I get into my car I slump back against the seat, the tension from having to socialize for so long leaving me exhausted. I pull out my phone to check the traffic home but it pings with incoming messages about six times before I even open the map app. I thumb over to my texts and see I've been added to a group. It looks like Kate, Lani, and Ophelia haven't wasted any time. I scroll down. As I read an amused smile grows on my face.

> KATE
>
> I was thinking about what Lani said—safety in numbers. We really do need to stick together during Operation: Nicole's Wedding. So this group chat is hereby declared a safe space for us bridesmaids to bash marriage, weddings & wedding planning, while also planning an "epic" bachelorette party & bridal shower for our dear, delusional friend Nicole, who we vow never to do the dubious honor of forcing into a peach-colored cocktail dress at any of our weddings.

KATE HAS RENAMED THIS GROUP: NEVER A
BRIDE(SMAIDS)
LANI

I'm in. You all are lucky you don't have to work
with her every day & have her talk up the
freaking UPS guy because she thinks 'we'd
have cute babies'

OPHELIA

Me too. Sorry Lani, that sucks :(BTW, since
she thinks we're already planning her
bachelorette party, do you think we need to
get on that?

KATE

Let's split up the tasks. Ophelia & Lani can do
the shower, Rosie & I can tackle the
bachelorette. Sound good?

I'm already in way over my head, but if you
don't mind holding my hand, I can do it.

LANI

Awesome idea, Kate. O & I will do the shower.
Kind of hard to start planning when she hasn't
even set a date.

KATE

She swore she'd have it in stone by the
engagement party—that's less than 3 weeks
away.

Less than three weeks. I may be an official member of this
Never-a-Bride group, but I'm still allowed to have fun. I start a
new text thread before I can do my overthinking thing.

Hey, you have dinner plans?

I force myself to switch back to the Never a Bride(smaids)
group instead of pathetically watching for Gus to answer my
text.

OPHELIA

BTW Rosie—Nicole wants you to send us all
pix of your engagement party dress

Why?

OPHELIA

I think she doesn't want us to dress too alike?

LANI

Seriously ladies, the UPS man. He's like 50!

I'll do it when I get home

KATE

That's rough

LANI

OTOH, our FedEx guy is a snack

My screen dings with a notification and I punch the little rectangle before it disappears.

GUS

I'm free. You want to meet up?

I do a little happy dance in the seat of my car. Dinner with Gus probably means sex after. I try to calm down and channel some of Lani's poise.

Sounds good.

GUS

Meet you somewhere? What do you feel like
eating?

I'm so full of tea and pastries that nothing sounds appealing right now. Maybe what I need is a little exercise before dinner. Sex first, food later. But how to phrase that in a text so I don't come off like a complete slut?

> Maybe I should come to your place and we could drive to dinner together. More fuel efficient.

GUS

Oh yeah? 😶 I'm home. Come anytime.

I definitely plan to.

CHAPTER 15

GUS

When I greet Rosie at the door, the first thing she does after crossing the threshold is kiss me and say, "Take off your shirt."

I spare one second of smugness that I didn't misinterpret her earlier text as a thinly veiled booty call, then waste no time whipping off my shirt and getting my hands underneath her little black dress. I kiss the lipstick off her mouth, chasing the taste of Rosie underneath. We've been apart for less than twenty-four hours, but it's a relief to be close to her again.

We don't make it past the living room, tumbling down onto my couch. Every touch burns hotter, takes us farther, faster since this isn't our first time. Rosie's sexy as hell and so pretty, her dress pushed up to her waist, her legs wrapped around my hips. I pull a couple of moves, unbuckling my jeans, getting a condom, while she touches my chest, her mouth open and wet. Then I pull aside her panties, plunge into her with nothing but latex in the way. She grips my back and cries out my name. We kiss and fuck and I hold off on coming until she's shaking under my fingers, riding out her own orgasm.

We're both a little sticky when we're done. She's flushed, even prettier now that she's got this glow in her cheeks. I smooth her dress back down but she scrunches up her face. "Ugh. My underwear is—" and she reaches down, pulling it off all the way. I swallow. Watching her shapely, bare legs as she wriggles out of her underwear gets me hot all over again. "Sorry, I just hate that feeling."

"I guess I got carried away." Should I apologize for the frantic pace?

"No, it's not that. It's just my weird thing. The sex was— yeah, that was what I wanted."

"Okay." I must have done something good in a past life if this sweet girl is coming to me for amazing quickies.

"Did you like it?" she asks, almost shyly.

"It was okay," I say, grinning so she'll know I'm joking. "Honestly, I've been thinking about doing that about every three minutes since you left here last night."

She digests that, then wraps her ruined underwear in what looks like a tissue and pops it into her purse. The fact that's she's apparently fine with going panty-less under her flimsy dress isn't lost on me, and I struggle to focus on her next words.

"Maybe you could put a shirt on and we could go get dinner? Not that I don't like this look on you." She eyes me up and down, which I find gratifying. She so likes my chest. I file the knowledge away for future reference.

In response, I pull my green polo back on, identical to my Pacifica Park uniform, but without the bougie embroidered palm tree logo. I add my local-pride 805 area code hat since I didn't bother to gel my hair today, and I'm good to go.

"You want me to drive?" I ask.

"Are you a good driver?"

"What man is going to answer that question with anything but hell yes?"

"Fair. I'm kind of a nervous passenger."

"You like to be in control."

"Pretty much."

"Believe it or not, hermosa, I figured that out about you already. But yes, I'm a good driver, and yes, if I screw this up, you can drive us both from now on."

"Deal."

We leave her hatchback parked on the street and get into the cab of my truck. I dust off the seat before she sits down, but it doesn't do much good. She doesn't complain, just asks where we should eat.

"Barbecue sound good?"

"Always."

I grin and head toward the center of town. I take it slow, conscious of my promise to drive carefully, aware that the privilege of driving Rosie could be rescinded at any moment. Even so, her dress is riding up her thigh a little, and her bare legs tease me. I put my hand on the soft skin above her knee and squeeze lightly.

The sex was so fast and hard before, I want more. I want to lay her down and feast on her until we're both wrung out. I shift in my seat, willing my erection away, promising myself there will be time for that later. I pray Rosie doesn't get sick of me before I've gotten to fill her up again and again.

She puts her hand over the one on her leg and laces our fingers together, turning my horny gesture into one that feels more intimate. I like it. She can be so hesitant sometimes. I don't know if she wants me to hold back, keep things purposefully casual, or if she wants to burn hot and fast before this so-called fling's time is up.

I park, shut the engine off, and wait for the verdict. "So, do I pass?"

"Excellent marks for driving, plus extra credit for foreplay."

"Foreplay, huh?" I tug her toward me. She climbs onto my lap to face me. I gather her close, telling myself I'm helping her avoid the horn. I belatedly remember she's not wearing any underwear as the scent of her sex, of our lovemaking, rises up between us. "Damn, I need you again." I kiss a line down her throat, sliding my hands up her thighs to palm her ass beneath her dress, soft and bare.

She kisses me back, grinds against me a little. "Not the best time or place." Her words are sensible, her voice is breathy, edging on needy.

Fuck. She's right. We're in full view in the parking lot. We don't want to give the other restaurant patrons a show. I groan and put a few inches between us. "Should we get dinner to go?"

"I like that idea," she says. We spend a minute breathing together, not kissing, not talking, letting our blood settle. I don't fully understand how Rosie can get me this hot. She's sexy, yeah, but maybe it's because I know she's not after more than what we have right here, right now. Sex, food, good company. She's not trying to spin this into something else—something neither of us wants.

We smooth ourselves down as best we can, and walk into the best barbecue joint in Ventura County holding hands. Even though this is just casual, I still have this need to touch her, to keep her close. I'm so...*into* her, for lack of a better word, that that it takes me a minute to realize someone from inside the dining room is calling my name.

"Gus! Gustavo Fernando Cuevas!"

Rosie's eyes widen as she looks over my shoulder and I turn around. A short woman with a haircut similar to mine, wearing a button-down shirt and long shorts walks up to us, smiling at Rosie. "Hi. I'm Gus's sister, Jess. Who are you?"

CHAPTER 16

GUS

My sister and I have always been close, but that doesn't mean I don't know she can be overbearing. I jump in before she can steamroll over Rosie. "Jess, this is Rosie. Rosie, my sister Jessica."

"Hi," Rosie says, in the reserved voice she uses when she meets someone new.

Jess glances between the two of us, down to our still-clasped hands. I resist the urge to let go. I'm not that much of an asshole.

"We just ordered. You're going to join us, right?"

"Um," Rosie says.

In theory, I wouldn't mind eating with Jess and my sister-in-law and my nephew, but Rosie didn't sign up for that. "We're actually getting takeout."

"Come on, you have to at least come say hi," Jess says, using her big-sister voice, the one I know is easier to give in to than fight.

"Sure." I give Rosie an apologetic smile. She just shrugs and we follow Jess past the host station into the dining room. It's crowded for a Sunday night, but I see two familiar faces at a table in the back. Unfortunately, they're not the faces of my sister-in-law and five-year-old nephew.

"Jess," I hiss, stopping in my tracks. "You didn't say you were here with Mom and Dad."

She glances at me, genuinely surprised. "Who did you think was here?"

"Carla and Eddie."

"They went to visit Carla's brother in San Diego this weekend. Not back yet. Come on."

I don't move. "If we come say hi, Mom will make us stay to eat."

"It's okay, we can stay," Rosie says quickly. "If you want to."

"You sure?" I'm fairly sure a spur-of-the-moment dinner with the parents falls outside the fling scenario.

Rosie nods, though her expression is more stoic than excited. Maybe, like me, she feels the opportunity for another round of sex slipping way. I shrug. "You have room for us?"

"We'll make room," Jess says, all smiles now that she's gotten her way. She leads us back to a four-top and cajoles a server into bringing an extra chair. My parents look surprised to see me, but they smile at Rosie.

"Mom, Dad, this is my friend Rosie. Rosie, Gustavo and Sandra Cuevas."

I let go of Rosie so she can shake my father's hand. When the greetings are over, she doesn't touch me again. I sit on the end, in the extra chair, half in the aisle, not really meant to be there. Story of my life. I've always felt like the extra chair in my family, the one no one really needs and doesn't understand and wouldn't really notice if it was gone. Probably why my parents are out with my sister for Sunday night dinner and it didn't even occur to them to ask me to come, too.

"So nice to meet a friend of Gus's, especially such a pretty one," my mom says, with all the subtlety of a bulldozer. "What do you do, Rosie?"

"I'm a doctor at Ventura Hospital," Rosie says. I watch her fiddle with her napkin and realize she's nervous. I'm so wrapped up with my own stuff, I'm not making this any easier on her.

"Rosie went to Santa Paula High, Mom. Class after me."

"I thought you looked familiar," Jess says. "I'm a year ahead of Gus, so we would have overlapped for a couple of years."

"Wait, weren't you on the mock trial team?" Rosie asks, her face brightening.

"Lead prosecutor two years in a row," Jess says. I experience that familiar mix of admiration and annoyance at my perfect older sister.

"I didn't join until I was a junior, but I remember watching a video of one of your trials to prepare for ours. You were so good!"

Jess beams and I have to control my urge to laugh. Of course Rosie and Jess would bond over something like mock trial. They're both smart girls.

"Now you're a doctor, that's wonderful," Mom says. "Gus, imagine what you could have done if you'd gone to college like your sister and Rosie."

"I did go to college, Mom, it just wasn't for me." If Rosie weren't here, I probably would have been out of my chair and out the door by now.

"He didn't even finish his associate's degree. But I guess you don't need college to be a gardener."

"Mom!"

I'm grateful to Jess for her sharp tone. I give her a hard time for being the favorite child, but she always has my back.

Rosie's voice, low but clear, cuts through my reflexive embarrassment. "I think Gus has just as much specialized knowledge as a doctor does. He knows everything about plants. He keeps them alive. He fixes them when they're hurt. He even makes hybrids that have never existed before. He's amazing."

There's a short silence. Mom's not sure what to make of Rosie's statement, but Jess smiles. "That's right. Gus is really good at what he does, Mom. I've told you, you need to go visit Pacifica Park. You'll see. It's not like he's spending all day mowing lawns. He's more like a scientist."

"Some scientist with dirt under his nails," Mom says, as if she doesn't want to give up having the last word.

The server breaks the awkward silence that follows by taking our orders. I order my regular, but I'm not even that hungry anymore. Getting the third degree from my parents instead of getting ribs and getting sticky with Rosie all over again back at my place—no contest.

Rosie orders the same thing I do, then glances at me, as if she's wondering why I'm not defending my job to my parents. She doesn't realize it doesn't matter how many times I explain what I do or how much I love it, my parents think I'm aiming low. They'd rather see me in an office job they can understand and tell their friends about, and nothing I do or say will change their minds. They've never once visited the garden.

"Jess teaches at Ventura High," I say, to change the subject.

"ESL and Freshman English," Jess says.

"Do you still live in Santa Paula?" Rosie asks.

"We do," Mom confirms. "Same house where I raised these two. We're comfortable there. Gustavo works at the bank in town, so it makes sense to stay. I miss seeing Jessica, and Gus, of course, now that they're set up in Ventura."

"Do your parents still live in Santa Paula?" my dad asks, his first contribution to the conversation. He's always been content to let Mom do the talking for both of them.

Rosie takes a sip of her water before responding. "My parents are both dead. My brother Jake lives in Oxnard, though."

"Sorry to hear that," Dad says gruffly.

"Yeah. Thanks." Rosie looks uncertain as to what to say next.

"Rosie's on vacation from the hospital for a little while. She's having a staycation," I say.

"A staycation? What's that?" Dad asks. "Something white people came up with?"

Jess laughs and I glance at Rosie, but she's laughing too. "It's when you stay at home but do things a tourist would do. Ventura's full of fun stuff to do that I'm too busy to take advantage of normally."

Like having hot sex, my brain supplies. Okay, maybe it's not my upstairs brain that came up with that one. "Like going to the beach," I say.

"Or museums," Jess suggests. "There's one on the Oxnard shore that's full of oil paintings of the ocean and model ships made out of bones. I took one of my classes on a field trip there last year. Really cool."

"I've always wanted to take a boat out to the Channel Islands," my mom says, startling me. "I've lived here my entire life and I've never been to the Channel Islands."

"There's always the Ventura Mission, and the Mission and Presidio in Santa Barbara," Dad says. He's a bit of a California history buff.

"These are all wonderful ideas," Rosie says, a bit sadly. "I wonder if I'll be able to fit them all in."

"Gus can go with you," Mom says. "Gus, find out when those boats go out to the islands. I think you get a better deal if you go during the week instead of the weekend."

"Mom, I have to work," I say, even though the idea of taking a day off to spend with Rosie in her swimsuit on a boat is tempting.

"It's okay," Rosie says quickly. "I'm also helping my friend with her engagement party. She's actually having it at Gus's garden. It's going to be beautiful."

"Really?" Mom looks confused. Before we go too far down that road again, I get the attention of the server and ask for the bill. When he brings it, I try to pay, but Dad, brusque and pretending to be offended, takes care of it for everyone.

"Rosie and I need to get going." She's been a saint to sit through the meal with all of its interrogations and awkwardness.

"Me, too," Jess says, grabbing her leftovers. "School night."

"Very nice to meet you, dear," Mom says.

"Nice to meet you, too," Rosie says. Then Mom pulls her into a hug, and Rosie's so taken aback she stumbles a little. I grab her elbow to steady her, and let her hand slide into mine again as she escapes my mom's embrace.

"Goodnight, Mr. Cuevas, Mrs. Cuevas," Rosie says. "Jess."

"I hope we get to hang out sometime," Jess says. "I have a lot of great dirt on this one." She jerks her thumb in my direction.

"Thanks, Sis," I say, plotting ways to keep my sister and Rosie apart.

We finally get outside, and I roll my shoulders, letting some of the tension roll off me.

"I am so sorry about that." I unlock the truck, open the door for Rosie to get in.

"It was fine," Rosie says.

"It was not fine. It was an ambush. I didn't know they were going to be there, and well, Jess is pretty forceful."

"I like her. I remember her from school now. Wasn't she the salutatorian or something?"

"Valedictorian."

"Wow."

"Yeah."

I start the truck and we head back to my place. I wonder if there's any way Rosie's going to want to pick up where we left off after being put through that.

"Do you think they liked me?" Rosie asks in that shy way

she has of making herself say something that she feels like she shouldn't say.

"Are you kidding? They were ready to trade me in for you. Then they'd have two kids they're proud of, a teacher and a doctor. My mom would literally kill to have a doctor in the family. Too bad Jess is more into books than bones."

"What do you mean? They're proud of you," Rosie says, but her voice isn't very confident.

"They're glad I support myself and have my own place and are probably shocked I haven't asked them for money in ten years. But beyond that, they think what I do is beneath me, or if not beneath me, beneath them. My dad's a loan officer and my mom's a secretary for an insurance agent. They have the two most boring jobs in the universe and they think being white collar is some mark of pride."

"I'm sure they just want you and your sister to be happy."

"Jess is happy being a teacher. I'd rather die than be stuck in an office staring at four walls all day. I'd go insane."

"Okay, I get it," Rosie says.

I belatedly realize I've been raising my voice, and of course she's not the one I'm angry at. It's not even my parents I'm mad at. I'm upset because I still care what they think. I love my job. I don't want it to change. But with Flora leaving, I may not have a choice.

"I'm sorry. This isn't about you." I pull into my driveway, reach over and tuck some of Rosie's hair behind her ears. "They loved you because you're awesome. Thanks for doing that—you didn't have to."

"It was actually kind of fun," Rosie says, "Your mom's a character, and your dad seems cool. Jess reminds me of my friend Nicole a little bit—bossy, always thinks she's right. Sadly, that's because she usually is."

"That's Jess."

"But next time it would be nice to have some notice so when

I see your parents I'm not reeking of sex and wearing no underwear."

I laugh. "Agreed. Though, if you're up for it, the no underwear thing could come in handy in about three minutes."

"Oh yeah?" She touches her tongue to her top lip, scoots across the seat toward me. "I'm up for it."

"What a coincidence—so am I."

CHAPTER 17

ROSIE

NICOLE

I just sent you the engagement pty guest list.
It's too long. You have to help me cut it down.

ROSIE

OK, I got it. How many people do we have
to cut?

Well there are about 200 names and I can only
invite 100, assuming a 25% decline rate.

You want me to help you cut 100 names off
this list?

Please, I can't do it by myself!

Shouldn't Ophelia help you with this? She
knows these people better than I do.

Yeah but she's working and I have to get the
invites out tomorrow at the latest. We're
cutting it close as it is.

...

PLEASE

I'M DESPERATE

I'll see what I can do.

Who's Dr. Farnsworth?

My orthodontist

Well, there's an easy cut.

He's also my dad's golf buddy.

You know what, why don't I just call you?

* * *

GUS

How's it going, hermosa?

ROSIE

Terrible. I was going to go for a run and to the bookstore and instead I've been on the phone with Nicole all morning discussing whether she should invite her Pismo Beach branch of the family to the engagement party.

Ha ha. You're a good friend.

Thanks.

If you want, I could keep you too busy to help her later.

How would you do that?

You could pick me up from work, we could get some food, go to a movie. No phones in the theater.

Genius. I'll take you up on that offer.

Sweet. Meet me at the Quonset hut around 3?

OK

* * *

I pull into the parking lot at Pacifica Park a little after three. My nerves are frayed from trying to help Nicole reduce her invitation list, and I desperately need a break from wedding stuff.

The garden isn't open to the public on Mondays, so I don't see a soul as I walk the gravel pathway past the cactus garden back toward the Palmetum, remembering the way to the Quonset hut.

I'm struck again by the profound peacefulness of this place. A breeze rustles leaves high above my head, contributing to the background noise of invisible birds and insects. There are a million shades of green everywhere, like being wrapped in a warm, green quilt of pure life. The garden itself feels like it's breathing.

I shake off the thought as fanciful. I envy Gus, though, getting to work somewhere so alive. The work I do helps keep people alive, but the environment is sterile, as it has to be. Here, oxygen comes from a tree, not a tube. I shiver. There's something about this place that turns me into a philosopher. I'm not sure I like it.

I see Gus and set aside my rudimentary philosophizing. He's talking to a co-worker, his back mostly to me. I get to observe him unnoticed. His Dickies and boots are streaked with mud, straw hat in one hand. He's wearing his work gloves today. The sun shines on his hair. The fade glints in the sunlight, probably wet from his sweat. The line of his nose is familiar; I'd recognize it anywhere.

The person Gus is talking to notices me and nudges Gus, who turns around.

"You're here! Rosie, this is Asai Ito. He's in charge of the cactus and euphorbia gardens."

"Hi." I wave.

"Hey, Rosie." Asai waves back. "Gustavo says you're heading to a movie."

"That's the plan."

"Cool, cool. Have fun. I've got to unload some barrel cactus we're moving."

"That sounds dangerous."

"Nah, I'm bigger than they are."

I laugh. Asai is indeed round and sturdy, similar to the barrel cactus itself.

"Well, good luck."

Asai heads down one of the paths, and Gus gives me a quick kiss on the cheek. He smells of sweat and earth. He smells like life. When I'm at work I smell like antibacterial soap and nitrile gloves. Not like death, exactly, but not like living things, either.

"Let me clean up and we'll head out."

"Okay. No rush."

"You want to come in? I'm just going to take a quick shower and change."

I think about Gus in the shower and bite my lip. "I better not."

He laughs. "You're right. I don't want to get in trouble for getting up to hanky-panky in the break room."

"I'll just walk around. There's still so much of the garden I haven't seen yet."

"You should check out the pond. We were working on the irrigation system there today. There are some beautiful *Nymphaea* in bloom."

"I have no idea what *Nymphaea* looks like, but I'll check it out."

"I'll find you."

He gives me another kiss on the cheek before he goes into

the hut. I touch my fingers to my face, feeling a bit like a teenager getting a kiss from her crush. I picture the garden map in my mind, remembering the pond is past the rose garden, so I head in that direction.

I pass the spot where I first met Gus, cradling his injured hand, swearing up a storm, and I smile. Is it bad that I like him this much? Isn't the whole point of this to have fun with no strings? I was supposed to take full advantage of vacation mode, clean out my system with plenty of amazing sex, then get back to business. It seems wrong, somehow, to feel this close to someone I'm not even going to see again in a few weeks.

Then again, there's no law against friends getting together and having no-strings sex once in a while. Just because every romantic comedy I've ever seen has proven that friends with benefits never works—either the friends end up hating each other or they end up realizing they're meant to be together—so what? Neither of those things has to happen with Gus and me.

I find the pond without much trouble. A woman in a park uniform works on covering up a pipeline with shovelfuls of dirt. She acknowledges my presence with a nod and keeps at her job. I scan the area, wondering which one is the plant Gus told me about.

"Excuse me, can you tell me where the *Nymphaea* is?"

"Right there." She points to a mass of floating green leaves interspersed with delicate white flowers a foot away. It could have bitten me, it's so close. "Also known as water lily."

"Oh. Thanks." I feel a little dumb. Maybe I should get a book on plants if I ever make it to the bookstore. Also, if Gus had just said water lily, I might have been able to find it on my own.

"You here to see Gus?" the woman asks.

Has he been talking about me to everyone at the garden? "Yeah. Hi. I'm Rosie."

"Michelle." She stops shoveling and I take a closer look at her. She looks strong, broad shoulders, blonde hair pushed under a Pacifica Park baseball cap. "Rose garden and head of irrigation."

"Gus said you were working on the irrigation down here."

"Having some problems with the recirculation. Should be fixed now."

"Ah." I'm so out of my element. Give me a sixty-year-old patient complaining of chest pain and nausea and I'm good to go. Ask me to identify something more obscure than a rose and I'm hopeless.

"You a landscape designer?" she asks, though her tone makes me suspect she already knows the answer.

"Nope. I'm a doctor. I don't know much about plants. Why do you ask?"

"Most of the girls Gus brings by the garden are landscape designers or landscape architects."

I stare at Michelle, feeling foolish and awkward, vaguely wondering what the difference between the two is. She pats down the earth at her feet and a minute later she's stowing her shovel onto the back of an electric cart.

"Enjoy the garden," she says, then zooms away.

I appreciate my newfound solitude and try to shake off the interaction. Of course Gus has brought other girls here, ones he actually has something in common with. We'd never have even met if I hadn't been forced to take this stupid vacation and Nicole hadn't forced me to come to this place.

Am I happy or sad that Nicole brought me here and that I met Gus? Things are getting complicated, and that's the last thing I want or need.

When he shows up, I'm staring at the water unseeingly.

"Hey, I found you."

"You did. Should we go?" I turn away from the pond.

"Sure. Everything okay?"

"I met Michelle. She showed me the *Nymphaea* and asked if I was a landscape designer. Or architect. What's the difference?"

"Architects have a different certification. More technical. But there's a lot of overlap."

"Ah. She seemed to think I might be one because you bring so many of them here." Do I sound jealous? I'm so not jealous.

Gus rolls his eyes. "Michelle doesn't know what she's talking about."

I feel better when he slips his hand into mine and leads me back to the parking lot. I'm distracted by a new set of smells—body wash and deodorant. Gus's hair is newly slicked back with gel, and he's wearing jeans and a button-down short-sleeved shirt. He points out interesting plants along the way, and I try to keep up with the commentary.

"That's a manzanita, they're native to California. Well, as near as we can tell."

"What does that mean?"

"There are different definitions of native when it comes to plants. Some people use the definition of 'lived here before Europeans settled.' But in California, the timeline of who went where and what they brought with them can be a little hazy."

"I had no idea."

"Plants are living history. They tell us a lot about how humans spread across the earth."

"I never thought about that before." We reach the parking lot and I'm feeling more settled, so I ask a bit playfully, "Should I drive this time?"

"Are you a good driver?" Gus asks with a smile.

"I think so, but you can be the judge."

We get into my car, leaving the truck behind. I'll drop Gus off later on the way home.

"So, what's the deal with Michelle?" I ask when we're

buckled up. I blast the A/C to take the edge off the afternoon heat.

"First, I have to say hello properly," Gus says. He cradles my face in his hands and kisses me thoroughly, until I forget anything but the feeling of his mouth. I open up to him, slipping my tongue between the seam of his lips, silently begging him to kiss me deeper, harder.

He obliges. When the kiss is in danger of veering too close to foreplay, we ease off as if mutually deciding to stop before we get sidetracked. He drops his forehead to mine.

"Hello," he murmurs.

"Hello." I sigh, a little lost. I don't know how to feel this good all the time.

"I guess we shouldn't just go back to my place," he says regretfully.

"I'm actually hungry. Thanks to Nicole, I skipped lunch."

"Then let's eat."

I love that Gus makes me feel desirable, but it's not like the only thing he wants from me is sex. He seems equally happy to spend time talking, eating, teaching me the difference between cactus and euphorbia. I'd never even heard the word euphorbia before I met Gus.

I drive toward Santa Barbara, the Pacific glinting gold on our left. Gus picks up the conversation. "Michelle's great with plants. Not so good with people. She told me today she's applying for director of horticulture position that's opening up at the garden."

"Is that bad?"

"Michelle has a very rigid view of Pacifica Park. She's worked here for a few years, but she's been visiting since she was a kid. She wants everything to stay exactly like she remembers it. She won't even plant any new cultivars in the rose garden unless she gets a lot of pressure from the board. If she becomes a director, she'll be making more of the decisions about the direction of the garden." He sighs and rubs his hand over his chin, a gesture I've seen him make only a couple of times before. "I'm afraid she'll keep things stagnant. I like to change it up, experiment. Sure, we keep a core inventory of plants. But we should be open to experimentation, hybrids, new cultivars. Plants change all the time. The garden should, too."

"Wow." I'm blown away by his passion and his clarity. He sounds like a politician giving a stump speech, not a local mayoral candidate, but, like, JFK or something. "You have to apply for that job."

"What?" He looks surprised. "What makes you say that?"

"You love the garden, Gus. You have a vision for it. Who better to be in charge?"

He's silent as we crawl along the PCH in early rush-hour traffic. When we finally get to the Garden Street exit he speaks.

"The woman who's leaving, Flora, really took me under her wing when I first started. She's mentioned a couple of times I should apply but—"

"You'd kill it, if that's what you're worried about."

He reaches over, squeezes my knee and flashes me one of the smiles that gives me a little thrill. "Thanks. But it's like there's a voice inside my head telling me the moment I make any plan further out than what I'm having for dinner that I'm stupid and my ideas are stupid. The voice sounds a lot like my mom, actually."

I pull into a parking lot on Anacapa. "Gus, listen to me. You made a success of your life, even without your parents' approval. You can do anything you want. I like your parents, but fuck them if they don't see how awesome you are. As for not making plans, hey, spontaneity is a good thing. Or so people keep telling me."

I park, turn off the engine. "But this is your career. You already make long-term decisions for the garden every day. You think about what your plants will need, how they're going to grow next week, next month, next year, in a decade. You'd plan the shit out of that garden if you put your mind to it."

I stop talking, kind of stunned all that came out of my mouth.

Gus looks surprised, too, as if he wasn't expecting me show such unfettered support for him.

"I can't believe you said, 'Fuck them,' about my parents."

My face warms. "Sorry?"

"No, that was amazing. You're amazing." He grins at me, then stares out the windshield, as if he's staring into the future. "I'll think about applying for the job."

"Okay."

He turns back to me. "I'm going to practice this making plans thing right now. Rosie, will you go out with me this weekend?"

"Um—"

"Damn, I just remembered we have this big event on Saturday so I'll be working overtime." Gus looks seriously bummed, then his face clears. "The week after. Saturday night, we'll do a full-on date night, okay?"

My palms go a little sweaty, but I nod yes. It's not like I already have plans. I didn't anticipate him taking my cheer-leader speech to heart so quickly.

We head for State Street and Gus wraps his hand around mine. In the garden, there had been no one around to see us holding hands. Here in the city's busy shopping district the public display of affection makes me feel like we're flaunting our together status and I almost pull away. Then I look around and see other couples strolling hand in hand. Some of them might be in Santa Barbara on vacation and I remember I'm not Dr. Rosie Snyder right now. I'm Vacation Rosie. She's the one sleeping with Gus. She's the one he wants to go on a date with.

Besides, I signed up for a fling, not for a boyfriend. Gus

knows I'm far from girlfriend material. When we get into the movie theater, I'll make him sit in the back row. A girlfriend would want to watch the movie, but a fling would want to make out the entire time, maybe see what else we could get away with. Making out during a movie is definitely a Vacation Rosie thing to do. Dr. Rosie is dead—at least for a little while longer.

CHAPTER 18

GUS

So what's up with you and Rosie? Are you a
thing?

We're friends.

Friends don't walk into a restaurant holding
hands looking like they just, um, got busy.

You seem to have already drawn your own
conclusion, so

Come on, I just want to know if I should invite
my future sister-in-law to Tia Linda's birthday
party next week

Hold. Up.

I've known the girl for a week.

And she's already met Mom and Dad and
she's a doctor and cute and clearly floats your
longboard.

Gross

Just saying

It's casual

Whatever. You're coming to Linda's birthday
tho, right?

Yes

Bring Rosie, bro

Maybe

* * *

I've got so much on my mind that Flora completely ambushes me on my way to the nursery the next day.

"Did you hear Michelle's applying for the job?" She falls into step beside me, easily matching her stride with mine. I was shocked to learn about a year after I started working for her that she was almost seventy. Now she's well past that, her snow-white hair invariably covered with a Pacifica Park green bandana. It hits me for the first time how much I'm going to miss her after she retires. Flora has given her entire life to this garden, and we're all the richer for it.

"I heard."

"So what are you going to do?" She's as blunt as my own mother, but the difference between the two is that Flora has my best interests at heart. Or I always thought she did. Now, I'm not so sure. Does she want me to apply for the job because she's afraid Michelle will unravel her legacy? Or does she really think I'm the best person for the job?

"I don't know." I told Rosie I'd think about applying, and I have been. Every time I think about taking that step, I stumble over all the reasons I'm under qualified. I imagine board meetings and budget fights and all the bureaucratic bullshit Flora has to put up with, and I just want to hold onto my pruning shears and my peaceful little corner of the garden.

The sound of our footsteps is loud in the stillness of the morning. Guests won't start roaming the grounds for another three hours. This is my favorite time of day, when the air is cool and damp and I still have enough energy to face all of the physical exertion the next eight hours will bring. I've never minded the physical part of my job. I'm strong, and using that strength in my work makes me feel good. Useful. Effective. Might I actually be more effective if I'm not the one down in the dirt all the time? Might it be better for the garden if I have a different role? Might it be better for me?

As if she can read my thoughts Flora says, "You know this garden better than anyone here. Besides me."

I smile.

"You know how to make it thrive. You know how resilient it is. You know it can change."

"I appreciate your faith in me, Flora—"

"It's not faith. I trained you myself, didn't I?"

"And I'm grateful, but—"

It seems she's not going to let me complete a sentence. "You're scared. You're scared to trade in your shovel for a computer. You think you'll be stuck behind a desk or in meetings all day."

"Aren't you?"

"I've been the head of this garden for twenty years. Back then we had half as many full-time gardeners. Half! I spent hours every day working in the garden beside them, trying to make my grand plans a reality. Over time, as the garden improved and attendance went up, we could afford more hires, and I didn't have to spend that time. Saved me from back surgery before sixty. But you're young, strong, smart. You don't have to do it the way I've been doing it. You can make the position your own. Sure, you're going to have to go to meetings. You have to be there to fight for your vision, to fight for the money, the time, the space. But the beauty of this job, Gus, is that the garden is your office. It's been mine for twenty years. It could be yours, too."

She strides off, leaving me at the entrance to the nursery before I can respond. I start my work mechanically, thinking hard. It takes me a few minutes to realize I'm overwatering my *Bismarckia nobilis* while wondering if it could be that simple. Can I make the job my own? Putting my ideas and my stamp on the garden would be a dream come true. It only comes down to putting aside my fears and making my own dream a reality. No one is going to do that for me. I have to do it myself.

At lunch, I pop into the main building, self-consciously wiping my boots off on the sisal mat at the front door. The office walls are pristine white, the dark wood floors glossed to a shine. Aradhana, the receptionist, smiles at me and tells me the director is in her office. I feel nervous, like I'm about to get a scolding from the principal, but Susan welcomes me with a smile.

"Hi Gus, I was hoping to see you today."

"You were?"

"We've got a couple of special events coming up I want to make sure are on your radar. There's a fundraiser for the children's hospital next week, and the week after, a private party. An engagement party, I think."

Rosie's friend Nicole's party. I smile, thinking of Rosie, realizing I'm excited to tell her later about what I'm about to do. She's going to be proud of me, and that makes me feel good.

"No problem. Tessa already went over the details of the fundraiser, we're all set." I talk over the wave of nerves that hits me. "I came by to let you know I'm interested in applying for the director position."

"That's great news," she says, after a short pause I can't interpret. "I'll email you the application today. The application portal is fairly easy to navigate, but let me know if you need any help."

"Okay. Thanks." Application portal? I have a computer, but I mostly use it for research and to track down hard-to-find cultivars. I try not to feel incompetent and back out of her office. When I emerge into the bright courtyard, Michelle's working in the euphorbias outside the office. Is it my imagination, or do her eyes narrow at me?

I go back to work with a strange sense of anticipation building in my gut. Having made the decision, all I can do now is do my best with my application, and the rest is out of my hands. I love Pacifica Park, and it would be exciting to get to steer it for a while. But for the first time, I also think about what it would mean to leave, to go to another garden, have a different job. I've been treading water for so long without even realizing it. I like my life, but that doesn't mean it couldn't be better. And if Michelle gets the job instead of me, I don't know if I can stay. Maybe I'd find someplace that makes me just as happy.

The afternoon drags on. I'm impatient to finish today. I want to find out if Rosie wants to get together so I can tell her about my decision. Her faith in me has a lot to do with me finally taking this leap. I text her as soon as I'm cleaned up.

You around?

I'm at Rincon!

Good for you. Want company?

Sure

It's only a few minutes drive to the Rincon in Carpinteria, and I have no trouble finding Rosie. It's a nice day but it's still a Tuesday afternoon in late September, and this stretch of rocky beach is otherwise empty. Most people are in school, or working, maybe stuck in traffic trying to get home. On a normal Tuesday Rosie would be working, too.

If not for her forced vacation and her random visit to Pacifica Park, we'd never have crossed paths. She'd never have gotten it into her head that we should have a fling. She's still acting like we have an expiration date, which used to seem like a plus to this arrangement. But the longer I spend with her, the more I don't want my time to run out.

I stroll up, putting thoughts of expiration dates and what-ifs out of my head. Rosie deserves to relax and have fun, not deal with my insecurities. The way she looks, perched on a brand-new beach chair in her sexy red swimsuit, nose stuck in a novel and floppy sun hat guaranteeing she won't be picking up too much sun, takes my mind in an entirely different direction.

"Whatcha reading?" I ask, plopping down in the sand beside her after sneaking a kiss onto her bare shoulder.

"It's a novel, an actual fiction book," she says, sounding incredulous. "I can't remember the last time I read a book just for fun."

"You made it to the library?"

"Well, the bookstore was closer to In-N-Out, so I picked up some books and lunch, too!"

"So efficient." The mention of food makes my stomach rumble. I eye her big straw tote. "You don't happen to have an extra double-double in that bag, do you?"

"In fact, I do. It's probably cold." She rummages around and produces the burger, a tray of fries, and a bottle of water.

"You're amazing. Cold In-N-Out is miles better than no In-N-Out. Thank you."

Her smile is brighter than the rays of sun bouncing off the Pacific.

She's still sipping on a shake, so we eat and she tells me about her morning talking Nicole off a ledge about the menu for the engagement party dinner, and I try to remember that

Rosie's not my girlfriend, even though all evidence points to the conclusion that she might be the perfect woman. She brought burgers to the beach, basically combining my two favorite things.

"What did you do today?" she asks, like we do this all the time. As if she actually cares how I spent my day.

"Same old, for the most part. But I did see Susan, the executive director of the garden. I told her I was going to apply for the director of horticulture position."

Her exclamation of pleasure rings in my ears and I laugh when she pushes up off her chair to join me on the sand and give me a hug. "Gus, that's fantastic. If they know what's good for them, they'll give it to you in a heartbeat."

"I don't know about that, but it feels good to try," I say. She just nods. I don't have to explain.

Eventually we go for a walk around the corner and I tell her some stories I have of surfing around here. We tiptoe around the tide pools and shiver when we get calf-deep in the surf. The sun seems to head toward the horizon much too fast and before long we have to pack up and drive in tandem back to my place.

I know things won't always be like this—she's going to get busy again when she goes back to work, and my hours will change if I get the director job, and...and...and I don't care. I like being with her. It's easy, if that makes any sense. I don't have to be someone else around her.

But I'm scared to ask for more. What if it turns out that I'm enough for a fling, but not for a real relationship? We've still got time. Maybe I can convince her that what we have could be the real thing.

* * *

Later that night we have sex twice, first time quick and dirty, well, quick and slippery, in the shower trying to clean up from the beach. The second time is after a dinner culled from leftovers in my fridge. We come together in my bed, slow and soft. I make her come twice with my mouth alone. Not that I'm keeping score.

Rosie's lying against my chest, and I know she's about to tell me she needs to get going. I tighten my arms around her, even though I know it won't do any good. "You don't have to go," I whisper, before she can say anything.

"You have to get up so early," she says after a pause. "I don't want to keep you up."

"I promise I won't wake you up in the morning."

"I better go anyway." She slides out of my arms. I can't shake the feeling she could slip out of my life as easily as she can slip out of my bed.

YOU AND A GUEST ARE CORDIALLY INVITED
TO CELEBRATE THE ENGAGEMENT OF
NICOLE TIFFANY WINESAP AND RICHARD JAMES KENDELL

SATURDAY, OCTOBER 12
7:00 PM

PACIFICA PARK
1 PACIFIC ROAD
CARPINTERIA, CALIFORNIA

FORMAL
NO GIFTS

CHAPTER 19

ROSIE

I'm having one of those mornings. The kind of morning where instead of hitting snooze on my alarm I turn it off and fall back asleep, and by the time I wake up I have to skip my shower and forget about blow-drying my hair, so I pull it into a haphazard ponytail, and the skirt I'd planned to wear turns out to have a broken zipper, so I have to rethink my entire outfit, and my car's low on gas but I have to have coffee so I decide to fuel myself instead of my car, and while I'm humming along on nervous energy and caffeine, I literally cross my fingers as I drive, hoping I won't run out of gas before I get to where I'm going.

The kind of morning where I wish I could go back to sleep and wake up tomorrow.

The kind of morning where I wish I could go back to sleep and wake up seventeen years earlier so that instead of it being the anniversary of the day my mother died, it's the day I don't screw up and my mom lives.

I make it to the cemetery coasting on fumes. I spot my brother's SUV in the lot and pull in next to it. Jake's waiting for me at the bottom of the gravel path that winds up the grassy hillside. He holds a bundle of paper-wrapped flowers in the crook of his arm, like a baby.

He looks the same as he did the last time I saw him, months ago, but it still startles me to see a grown man instead of a little boy. He's two years younger than me, and a head taller. He looks so much like Dad, whose grave we will also visit today, neat and tidy next to Mom's.

I hug him and he squeezes me back lightly. Jake isn't known for small talk and I can't think of a thing to say. He starts walking and I fall into step beside him.

We've done this every year for seventeen years, but I always have trouble remembering exactly where Mom's grave is. Maybe it's the monotony of the stones. The cemetery is pretty new, as these things go, and the simple gray slab grave markers peel out in orderly, identical rows. Jake seems to know where he's going.

"Feels like we just did this," I say, when we finally reach our destination. Twenty rows up, four plots to the left. I counted.

Iris McGill Snyder. Jake places the flowers—irises, of course, white ones—on her grave. We didn't bring anything for Dad's grave, but he wouldn't have minded, as long as we take care of Mom. I brush some dirt off the front that's obscuring part of his name. Robert Jacob Snyder.

"Yeah, it does," Jake says. He clears his throat. "Don't you feel bad that the baby isn't mentioned?"

"Dad didn't want it to be." He knows this, but I say it anyway. "We remember it."

"Her, not it," Jake says, surprising me.

"Her." Something about the iris bouquet triggers my memory. "Daisy. Mom told me she wanted to name her Daisy if she was a girl."

"She did?" He looks at me as if I've insisted the moon landings were a hoax. "Why didn't you tell me?"

"I'm sorry, I think I blocked it out. It just came to me."

For a second I'm worried that he's going to berate me for keeping something like that from him, but in the end he just looks sadder than he did before.

"I'll bring daisies next year," he says quietly.

My heart's usually too atrophied to fully appreciate how devastated Jake is every time we do this. Today I'm thawed enough to notice the groove between his eyebrows, the hunch of his shoulders. He was only eleven when Mom died. He lost her and our baby-sister-to-be in one awful day, then got stuck with a ghost for a dad and an older sister who did the best she could until she escaped to college. He got the rawest end of the raw deal that was our childhood, and I've never known how to make it up to him.

We walk back down the hill, hands in our pockets, pilgrimage complete for another year.

"Your car running okay?" he asks when we get to the bottom.

I smile faintly. That's Jake language for "how are things going in your life?"

"It's running great. Thanks." I don't mention that I'm low on gas.

"You should bring it by my work to get the oil changed. It's probably overdue."

"Good idea."

"Hey, I have to get going, but I need to tell you something first."

I search his face for an indication of what he might be about to say. Good news? Bad news? He's as stoic as ever. "What is it?"

"My girlfriend, Becca, she's, uh, pregnant. And we decided to get married. Just at City Hall. The baby's due in November."

I blink a couple of times. "You're getting married. And having a baby. With someone named Becca." I take a deep breath. "Jake—I didn't even know you had a girlfriend!"

"Apparently I'm not the best communicator. Becca says it's because I'm traumatized. About Mom and everything. She's got me going to a counselor. You know, like a therapist?"

I nod and try to contain my astonishment. My brother's just shared more information about himself in the last thirty seconds than in possibly his entire adult life. He's going to be a *dad*. He's going to *therapy*. What is happening right now?

"Anyway, Becca's great. You'll really like her. She's smart, like you."

"I'm sure I will like her if I ever get to meet her." My consternation manifests in sarcasm.

He cringes a little. "Okay, okay. We'll get together. I promise. It's just, you're always so busy with work. I don't want to bug you."

"I know I work a lot, but I can have a life outside of work." Doesn't matter that until a few days ago I would have argued the exact opposite. My brother's got an entire life he's kept separate from me, and it's got me defensive and off-kilter. I'm scared that I'm losing the only family I have left, and that makes me reckless enough to make a promise. "I'll make time for you, if you give me a chance."

"I'll try to do better if you will."

"Fair enough." Classic sibling bargain complete, I give him another hug while forcing the tears that suddenly well up to stay put for another few seconds. "Congratulations. I'm so happy for you."

"Thanks, Rosie. I'll see you soon?"

"Definitely."

As he climbs into his car and drives away I notice that his shoulders have dropped and the lines on his forehead have smoothed out. I wonder if part of his stress was from psyching himself up to tell me his news. Am I such a terrible sister that he was nervous about telling me he's got good things in his life?

I should get in my car, too, but I linger, fingering my keys in my pocket and glancing back at the hillside cemetery. I want to go back to Mom, sit down and have a good cry. Part of me worries if I start crying I might never stop.

I'm so happy for Jake. I assumed he was like me—unable to have a real relationship with someone. Afraid to have kids. But maybe I'm not a total failure of a sister if he's embarking on a committed relationship, looking forward to parenthood, and going to therapy, no less.

There's a not-too-subtle voice in my head telling me that therapy wouldn't be a bad idea. Physician, heal thyself and all that. It's not like I don't believe that therapy can be helpful—exactly the opposite.

It's just that I don't deserve to be helped.

I don't go back to Mom's grave. I whisper aloud the words I've said about a million times in my head and my heart for seventeen years.

"I'm sorry, Mom. I'm sorry I couldn't save you. I'm sorry I wasn't good enough to keep you alive."

I wipe away the single drop of saline that's strong enough to escape tear duct lockdown, get in my car, and get back on the road.

I make it about a third of a mile before the car starts losing power. I pull over onto the shoulder in time to hear the engine conk out. My car's out of gas, and I'm out of luck. I clunk my head against the steering wheel and jump when I accidentally honk the horn.

Shit. I'm in the middle of an agricultural corner of the county, orange groves on one side of the road and tilled farmland on the other. I have no idea how close the nearest gas station is. I'd call AAA but I vaguely remember letting my membership lapse. I refuse to call Jake and make him late for work. Nicole would help, but she's over an hour away.

Gus said he wasn't going into work until later today.

I sigh. It's definitely not in the fling job description, but I call him anyway. I can't stay here forever, even if part of me thinks being stranded on an empty stomach is no less than I've earned.

Gus is understanding and says he'll be there in half an hour, which only makes me feel worse. Why is he so freaking *nice*?

"Stay in the car and lock the doors. It's not safe to stand on the shoulder."

Since only one car has passed me since I've pulled over, I'm not exactly worried, but I tell him I will.

"By the way, how do you like bowling?"

The change in topic throws me a little. "Uh, it's okay, I guess."

"Just thinking about our date. Next Saturday, remember?"

"Right. Saturday. Bowling. Got it."

"Stay put, hermosa."

Gus may only give a fuck about me because we're fooling around, but he's coming to my rescue anyway.

I dig through my purse and find a Kind bar, aka breakfast, then open my text app to see several missed ones from my fellow Never a Bride(smaids) and a conversation in progress.

LANI

Heads up—Nicole's been ranting around the office talking about our plus-ones for the engagement party. I'm assuming none of us has one?!?

KATE

I'm going solo

OPHELIA

Same

LANI

The woman is a lunatic. She just signed a
huge deal to license some of her designs for
an exclusive wallpaper line and all she can talk
about is this stupid party in the park.

OPHELIA

Despite Pacifica Park's name, it's actually
more of a botanical garden. But yeah.
Priorities.

KATE

That's awesome, Lani. I bet you had
something to do with making that deal
happen, am I right?

LANI

Well, I did approach the firm and put together
the agreement. But our lawyer vetted it.

KATE

Oh, well if that's all... :-P You're a rock star,
babe. Nicole better know how lucky she is to
have you on her team.

LANI

I don't need thanks, just need her to shut up
about wedding stuff once in a while.

OPHELIA

Congratulations on the deal, Lani. Kate's right
—Nicole better treat you right. You tell me if
she doesn't and I'll yell at her.

KATE

You don't yell.

OPHELIA

I only yell at the people I love. It's a very short
list.

I bite my lip and jump into the fray.

> I second that—you are a rock star, Lani. And I
> don't envy you on the front lines of Nicole's
> special kind of crazy.

LANI

Rosie! How's your staycation? Got a tan yet?

I laugh and glance down. I have gotten some sun, but I haven't been anything close to tan since college.

> Still working on it. But the staycation is OK.
> Except for the part where I forgot to get gas
> and am now stuck on the side of the road.
> Routines are a good thing!

KATE

Oh no! Did you call AAA?

> A friend is coming to help.

LANI

Your staycation "friend?"

> His name is Gus. No quotes needed.

LANI

jk girl. You're not bringing him to the party,
tho are you?

That stops me. When Nicole first mentioned the engage-ment party, it never occurred to me I'd even have anyone to possibly accompany me. An image flashes through my head, me in my emerald green dress, Gus by my side. He'd probably look beyond adorable in a suit and tie. I swallow. It doesn't matter. I don't get to have that, and who's to say he'd want to be my date, anyway?

> I didn't think she had room on the guest list for
> plus ones.

> Not that I'd bring anyone, of course.

It feels weird to lie in a text. It's pointless and stupid and I wish I could take it back. As much as these girls aren't interested in relationships, I know they wouldn't care if I actually wanted to bring someone I really liked. But that's just it. Do I like him? Or is the novelty of great sex with a good guy masking itself in erroneous feelings?

LANI

Perfect. Just wanted to make sure we're all on the same page.

I glance up at the sound of an engine. Gus's truck pulls up alongside me. He rolls down his window and grins at me. I do the same. The fresh air feels nice after being trapped in the car.

"Fancy meeting you here, hermosa." He looks absolutely delighted at being able to help me out.

"Fancy that," I respond, my chest tight with some unfamiliar emotion. I glance down at my phone, then click the screen off.

I have no idea what page I'm on anymore.

CHAPTER 20
ROSIE

The second week of my staycation goes by even faster than the first. Even though he's working most of the weekend, Gus invites me to watch a movie Sunday afternoon at his place. Because it's been a couple of days since we had sex, the movie, understandably, goes unwatched. One guess as to how we pass the time instead.

A month ago, I would have thought it impossible to fill up a workweek without work, but I find myself busy nearly every minute of the day. Mostly I'm helping Nicole with engagement party stuff, which causes me to meet her on her turf in Santa Barbara. Since Pacifica Park is on the way home, I end up stopping in at the garden a couple of times, enjoying the times I spend wandering around on my own almost as much as the times I have Gus as a tour guide.

I manage to squeeze in a few personal errands, too. Some things I try go better than others—after getting my first pedicure and seeing how elegant my toes look painted shell pink, the ladies at my neighborhood nail salon have a customer for life. But my attempt at soaking up culture is stymied by the fact I had no idea that many museums are closed on Mondays, except when they're closed on Wednesdays.

Gus is amused at my frustrated attempt to visit Santa Barbara's art museum on its weekly closed day and promises to take me another time.

He reminds me of our upcoming Saturday night date nearly every time I see him. Since we spend most of our time together eating, talking, and having sex, I'm not really sure how Saturday's going to be any different, but I promised him. I only hesitate for a second when he asks for my address so he can pick me up, old-school style. I've avoided having him to my place, but I can't think of any rational reason he shouldn't know where I live. The lines are blurring, but luckily I have the Never a Bride(smaids) to keep my head on straight.

* * *

KATE

Found my dress! Let me know if you think it meets Nicole's guidelines of 1) "in the spirit of romance and new beginnings" and 2) not too similar to Rosie's.

LANI

Hot

OPHELIA

Your legs are going to look amazing in it!

So gorgeous

KATE

Thanks. It took 3 solid hours on Melrose, but I figure I can wear it to any holiday parties I get invited to this winter

OPHELIA

Definitely. I approve! Does it have pockets?

LANI

You and your pockets

                      Mine does!

KATE

No, maybe I could get someone to put some
in for me.

OPHELIA

Haven't designers figured out that all dresses
need pockets by now?

LANI

Pockets are a millennial cliché

                      But so useful

LANI

Dammit. You're right :-P

KATE

Wish we all lived closer sometimes. You could
come with me tonight to this mixer one of my
clients is having that I can't get out of.

OPHELIA

But how would I binge the rest of The Witcher
if I was actually out interacting with humans?

KATE

Ugh, I'm so jealous. Henry Cavill is my jam.

LANI

I'd go with you, Kate, but my Saturday night's
booked with going over our holiday orders.
Good thing Nicole didn't schedule the
engagement party during our busiest season.

LANI

Oh wait.

                Sorry you have to work, Lani

LANI

It's OK. What do you have going tonight,
Rosie?

Bowling?

KATE

You're not sure?

It was Gus's idea

LANI

So your fling is still…flinging?

We're having fun

LANI

Girl, I have nothing against fun. You better
have enough fun for all 4 of us, sounds like.

I'll try

I'm used to the knock on my door from food delivery drivers, but tonight the person knocking isn't bringing me Thai noodles. When I open the door I see that Gus has brought me something, though not takeout. He steps inside, presses a small potted plant into my hand, and kisses my cheek in one svelte move. I lean into his warmth and scent, which is more delicious than Thai noodles. And I *really* love Thai noodles.

"What's this?" I ask, holding the pot tightly, as if it might slip out of my grasp and shatter all over my white tile floor if I'm not careful.

"That is a *Dracaena draco*. A dragon tree. They are very easy to take care of and very difficult to kill."

"Sounds perfect for me."

"I had a feeling you'd want something low maintenance."

I glance around the entryway of my condo, trying to figure out where to put it.

Gus takes it back gently, then wanders through to the kitchen. My phone buzzes and I glance down at my notifications. The Never-a-Bride(smaids) conversation is proceeding without me on the merits of bowling, so I figure it's okay if I catch up later. I follow Gus, wondering how he'd react if he knew I considered myself a Never a Bride. If he were a normal guy, he'd probably be relieved. But Gus isn't a normal guy. For instance, instead of the traditional, and obvious, bouquet of roses to kick off our date, he brought me a dragon tree.

"I also had a feeling this might be your first houseplant. It just needs some sun and a bit of water now and then."

"How much is a bit? And how often is now and then?"

He sets the pot down next to the window that overlooks the parking spot behind my unit, laughing a little. "Relax. If the soil's dry, empty your water glass on it. Seriously, Rosie, you can't hurt it."

He turns around, glancing around my kitchen. I notice for the first time how good he looks tonight. His dark jeans hug his muscular legs and his lighter denim button-down shirt is rolled up to the elbows. He's traded his work boots for worn-but-shined brown cowboy boots, and his hair looks freshly trimmed, the fade sleek and neat.

"Nice place. How long have you lived here?"

"Two years."

Something—surprise?—flashes across his face.

"It's a little plain." I try not to sound defensive, but I'm sure he's thinking I'm the world's most boring person. There's not much in the kitchen that reflects me, not even a cookbook, since I never cook. Unlike the front of his fridge, cluttered with family photos and the detritus of his life, the only thing on mine is my gym's Zumba schedule.

"It's very...clean." He kindly refrains from voicing the notion that maybe I'm a serial killer based on the lack of personal effects.

"Thanks."

"So, you want to get going? Can you wait a bit to eat? I thought we'd do our activity first."

"Um, sure." I sort of thought he might try to skip to the sex part of the evening, but it seems he's adhering to the date night script, even if he's adding his own twists. I grab my purse and dab on some lip gloss.

"Am I dressed okay for bowling?" I'm wearing jeans, a loose floral top and Toms. I brushed my hair shiny and left it loose. I've gotten so much more sun than usual this week there are new freckles across the bridge of my nose, but I didn't bother to cover them up with makeup. It still feels like summer, even if we're almost into the second week of October.

"You're dressed perfectly for bowling," he says, eying me openly up and down. His mouth curves into an approving smile. I don't need him to validate either my outfit or the way I look. Still, I won't lie and say it's not nice to be appreciated. "But we're not going bowling."

"Oh, thank God." I lock the door behind us and head for his truck in the visitor's parking space. "I'm the world's worst bowler."

He grabs my hand and gives me a wicked grin. "Excellent. How do you feel about mini-golf?"

CHAPTER 21

ROSIE

The mini golf course is a local landmark, with its signature cotton-candy pink castle clearly visible from one of the busiest freeways in California, as good as a lighthouse for marking two-thirds of the way between Los Angeles and Santa Barbara.

"I've never been here before," I admit as we pull into the half-full parking lot. "I used to think this was a real princess's castle." It represented something as magical and unattainable to me as going to Disneyland. Growing up there was never money for anything as extravagant as a family mini golfing excursion. I was in college before I went to Disneyland for the first time with Nicole.

"It is a princess's castle," Gus says seriously. "Tonight, you are la princesa. You can have anything your heart desires."

I laugh, my cheeks coloring. No one has ever said that to me before. I've spent my life pointedly not contemplating what my heart desires, because what it wants most can never come true. But tonight seems almost magical, one wish about to be filled. I almost think Gus could do it—he could make my every desire come true.

I put my hand in his, Princess Rosie and her escort, and we

go inside the seventies-era brick building where we're fitted with golf clubs and tiny pencils.

"You haven't been here, but you have played mini golf, right?" he asks as we line up behind a group of middle school girls who shriek and laugh as they try to get their golf balls through the first hole.

"Once or twice. I'm a little better at this than at bowling."

"Want to make a wager on the outcome of the game?"

"You want to bet on mini golf?"

"Yeah. Winner of this round gets a favor from the loser. Anything they want."

"Anything?" My eyebrows lift. "High stakes."

"Okay, I should have known that would be too open-ended for you. How about if you win, you can ask me for anything you want. If I win, I get to sleep over at your house tonight."

"What?"

Gus steps closer to me, his face inches from mine. I can see the rough of his five o'clock shadow on his cheeks and chin. His teeth are white and his lips look soft. If I didn't know him so well, I might have thought he was trying to intimidate me, but I know he just wants me to really listen to him when he speaks, his voice soft and low so only I can hear.

"Here's what I want, hermosa. I want to beat you at mini golf and win you an ugly stuffed animal in the arcade. I want to take you for the best fish you've ever eaten and splurge on dessert. I want you to invite me to your place, and I want to make love to you in your bed. I want your sheets to smell like us. I want to sleep with you. All night." He licks his lips; I can't tear my gaze away from the pink tip of his tongue. "In the morning I want to lick you until you come again and then go back to sleep until noon. Eventually we'll get coffee and eggs and take a walk on the beach. Then, if you're really and truly sick of me, I'll say goodbye."

I say the only words that come to mind. "Holy fuck."

"You're up first." Gus takes a step back, gestures with his club. I stumble as I lean down to balance my hot pink ball on the tee.

"Everything okay, hermosa?" Gus can't keep the smirking smile off his face.

I glare up at him. "You play dirty, Gustavo Cuevas."

He puts his hands up in surrender. "Hey, I do what I gotta do."

I stand up and steady myself in front of the tee. I line up my club. I empty my mind. I breathe. I take a swing and make contact. The ball shoots up the ramp, over the other side, bouncing off the walls of the course, and comes to rest at the very edge of the hole. As Gus and I run to inspect my shot, the ball wobbles a little and falls into the hole. I whoop and pump my fist.

"A hole in one! How do you like them apples?"

Gus groans in faux defeat. "You're a ringer! Oh man."

I laugh and point my club at him. "Your turn."

We're off to the races, with him taking three shots to my one on the first hole, tying with two each on the second, and so on until it comes down to the very last hole.

We're tied, so if I can get fewer strokes to get my ball in the big clown's mouth at the end of the course, I'll win. And if he wins, he'll get to stay over. We've never spent the whole night together. We could have. But each time it comes up, I extricate myself as gracefully as possible. I don't want him to feel like I don't want to because of him. It's not about him. It's about me. It's about feeling like this vacation fling has already gotten way too out of hand. It's about feeling like I never want this vacation to end if it means I don't get to see Gus any more.

I take my shot. Another hole in one, but I take no joy in it.

He's about to take his shot.

"Wait! What happens if we tie?"

Gus strokes his chin. "Rematch?"

I laugh. Going through the course all over again doesn't sound that bad. I've never had so much fun playing a game in my life. Gus managed to take my competitive instincts and use them for good. It's kind of scary how well he knows me.

"Okay. Good luck."

"Yeah, right." His first hit ricochets off the clown's chin, but he gets it in on his second try. "Looks like you get anything you want, hermosa."

I'm terrified, but I owe it to him to be honest.

"Um, what you said sounds good. Can we do that?"

His eyes get wide. "Seriously?"

It's sad but not surprising that he doesn't think I'd want that beautiful picture he painted of the two of us to come true, at least for one night.

"Seriously." I don't want to want it, but I do.

He kisses me then, pulling me tight to him, until our golf clubs clatter together and we break apart, remembering we're in public. "All right. Let's do it. Tomorrow's Sunday, we can spend the whole day together being lazy." Gus's phone buzzes and he checks it while I return our clubs. He's frowning when he looks up from the screen.

"Everything okay?"

"Yeah. It's only Jess. My Aunt Linda's birthday party is Friday and she keeps asking me if you're coming."

"Oh."

"It's okay, you totally don't have to go." We head inside the arcade, lit up with multicolored lights. Taylor Swift blasts out of the speakers and the noise of twenty games being played at once by rambunctious teenagers makes my head spin.

I don't know what to say. Our relationship isn't the kind that's supposed to include family functions.

"I'd rather have you all to myself anyway," he says before I can respond. "Jess just wants a chance to tell you embarrassing stories about me."

"I'll bet there are a lot," I say, to lighten the mood.

"Hey!" he protests, then shrugs. "Okay, yeah. I bet your brother has plenty of dirt on you, too."

I freeze. It never occurred to me that Gus and Jake might meet, let alone talk about me. Jake does have dirt. He knows my darkest secret, my biggest shame. Gus has no idea what I've done. If Jake told him about what happened with Mom, he wouldn't want to finish out our three weeks together.

I look around at the groups of regular, seemingly happy people playing games and whiling away their Saturday nights with the people they love. I'd forgotten for a little while that I don't get to have this. Gus deserves to be here with someone less fucked up—a woman he can bring to family parties, one who lets him sleep over without having to wager for it, one who wants more than a fling.

Suddenly, the prospect of spending the rest of the evening being romanced by Gus makes me ill.

"What's wrong? I'm joking."

"I know. Sorry, it's fine." I put my hand on my stomach. "I'm just hungry."

"Let's go to dinner, then. Rain check on the stuffed-animal winning."

"Right." I let Gus lead me back to his truck, but I know that we'll never come back here. My reign as Princess Rosie is over. The sooner I let Gus go, the sooner he can find the girl who's meant to be his queen.

CHAPTER 22
GUS

Despite her totally awesome win at mini golf, Rosie is kind of quiet on the drive to the Oxnard shore. Our destination is a really great fish market that has a small upscale restaurant attached. Rosie doesn't need things to be fancy to have a good time, but I think she'll like this place.

Plus, I have no problem being with her somewhere dark and intimate. I relax as we talk quietly, falling into her dark brown eyes, happy to simply exist near this woman. Another part of me is intensely aware that she's agreed to let me spend the night. When I let myself think about it, I'm as eager as if it's our first time. I don't want to blow it out of proportion, but if I can get Rosie to see what we're building here is too good to throw away, then we might have a shot at a real future together.

After a lifetime of being told my plans for the future suck, I'm ready to start trying again. I'm ready to build something that's going to last, that's got room to grow.

Still, I know Rosie's not ready to hear any of that. The last thing I want to do is scare her away, so I keep to light topics—the latest projects we're working on in the garden, the fact that I have the interview for the director position in a few days. We brainstorm some possible interview questions that I can practice ahead of time. When I start to get nervous thinking about the interview, I ask for the latest download on Nicole's wedding plans.

"Apparently even the engagement party has to have a theme, so Nicole decided on 'Starry Romance.'"

I snort into my scallops. "What does that even mean?"

"I have no idea. This fish is outrageously good."

"Want a scallop?" I set one on her plate before she can answer. "It sounds like a prom theme."

"Did you go to your prom?"

"Oh sure." I watch her try the scallop, not hiding my grin at her moan of pleasure. "Took Scarlet Ramirez."

"I remember her—she was a Goth girl, right?"

"I think she's a dental hygienist now. What about you? Did you go to prom?"

Her expression darkens. "I didn't do anything fun in high school."

"I remember you being really smart and really quiet."

"You do?"

"Sure. I remember feeling like a complete idiot because I was the only junior in a class of sophomores, but you smiled at me. It was like you wanted me to feel like a part of the class."

"I remember you, too," she says, surprising me. "I remember being intimidated by you because you had a mustache."

"Ah, I remember that 'stache." I laugh. "I was trying to seem older, but I'm pretty sure I just looked like a kid with a fake mustache."

"Wait, it wasn't fake?" Rosie jokes.

I nudge her calf under the table with my foot, put another scallop on her plate.

"Well, you'd look good with facial hair now. I mean, more than your five o'clock shadow."

"You think so?" I waggle my eyebrows at her. "You want me

to grow a beard? It would make things more interesting when I go down on you."

"Gus, stop." She blushes, even though no one in the restaurant is paying us any attention.

"Sorry, hermosa. I'll grow a beard if you want."

"Really?"

"I told you—whatever your heart desires."

She falls quiet. The server delivers our dessert—dark chocolate something and two spoons. Rosie hadn't wanted to order anything but I know she's a sucker for chocolate.

"You're spoiling me," she says quietly, looking at the dessert instead of me.

"You're fun to spoil."

"What does that mean?"

"You don't expect it. That makes it fun to give you things. Everyone should get spoiled once in a while. Especially you, princess. You work so hard taking care of everyone else, you forget to take care of yourself."

"I'm trying," she says softly. "That's what this whole stupid vacation has been about. Trying to put myself first. It's not easy."

"Takes practice. Start with a spoonful of this," I point to the dessert, "add some hot sex, throw in a massage. We'll make a hedonist of you yet."

She laughs, takes a bite of the chocolate, closes her eyes and whimpers in pleasure. The sound goes straight to my cock.

"See, you're a natural."

She opens her eyes. They're dark with pleasure. I need to see them that way underneath me in bed. I need to see them that way every night, every morning. I need to know that no matter what happens when she goes back to work, we're going to stay together, stay strong.

I want her to let me spoil her for the rest of her life.

I can't say any of that. I motion to the server for the check and push the dessert plate toward Rosie.

"You don't want any?"

"I'm not hungry for that, hermosa." Her eyes widen as she gets my meaning. I take it as a good sign that she's done by the time I tuck my wallet back into my jeans. Once back in the truck, I can't help but kiss her. She tastes like chocolate and my blood's so hot I don't know if I can make it to her bed after all. I squeeze her tits through her flimsy top; she gasps when I thumb the tips of her nipples through her bra.

"Gus. Fuck."

"Yes."

"Wait. We can't do this here."

I drop my hands onto the steering wheel. "Sorry. You're just —you're better than dessert."

She smiles at me, but it's crooked, like she's trying not to frown. "Drive fast."

CHAPTER 23

GUS

Rosie's place isn't far and I manage to get us there without breaking any laws. Her condo is so clean and orderly that the dragon tree in its humble terra-cotta pot stands out like a splotch of brown paint on a white canvas. This sterile, unlived-in space doesn't reflect the Rosie I've come to know.

The Rosie I know brims with life and energy and passion. I suspect she's thrown all of that energy into her work and kept very little of it for herself. That's great news for her patients, for the community that depends on her hospital to provide care to a huge swath of the population. But while Rosie's healing everyone else, who's taking care of her?

Tonight, that's all me. Her pleasure is my one and only objective. It's just lucky for me that touching her, tasting her, making her come over and over again makes me feel incredible, too.

Once we get inside, I make an effort to slow down. I ask for a tour and she pauses in the act of slipping out of her shoes.

"Um. This is the downstairs. Laundry room over there, half bath, open-plan kitchen-slash-living room." She picks up her shoes, carries them with her. She's probably going to put them away in her closet when we get to her room, adorable neat freak that she is.

"Nice." I take the shoes out of her hand, drop them carelessly, and back her up against the nearest wall. She sighs into my shoulder when I start kissing her ear. "Open plan kitchens are really popular."

"What is happening right now?" she asks, arching her head back so I can kiss my way down her neck.

"You're giving me a tour." I suck on her collarbone lightly, release the tender skin, run my tongue over it to sooth the mark. "You're a great tour guide."

"Thanks." She sounds drunk, even though we each only had a single glass of wine.

"What's upstairs?" I nuzzle her breasts through her top, then give up the pretense and just pull it up and off her, leaving her in a sheer black lace bra. Her nipples show dark through the thin material. I lean down to lick them, then stop when she doesn't answer. "What's upstairs, Rosie?"

She groans. I don't resume coaxing her nipples into hard peaks until she starts talking again, her voice strained. "Guest bedroom, guest bath. My bedroom has a walk-through bathroom attached."

I pause long enough to say, "Great for resale," then start peeling the bra down over her tits with my teeth. Her breasts spill out heavy and glistening with my saliva.

Breathless, she says, "That's what the Realtor told me."

"They were right." I step back and admire my handiwork. Rosie's eyes are closed and her pink mouth is open. Her bra is a black underline, punctuating her breasts. She looks sexy as hell, barefoot, her belly swelling softly over the top of her jeans. "Maybe you should show me your bedroom now."

Her eyes fly open and I watch them focus, the realization that she's half-naked in her living room filtering into her consciousness. I consider it a victory when she simply turns and walks up the white-carpeted staircase.

I toe off my boots and leave them behind, then bound up after her, adjusting myself on the way. At the top of the stairs a light turns on in the first room on the left. Rosie's room. I pause outside the threshold. This is the holy grail. Two weeks in which we've had sex two dozen times and I've never been this close to her inner sanctum.

I step inside, vaguely relieved that her room isn't as lifeless as the rest of her place. There are some colors besides white, at least. The bed is neatly made with soft-looking block-printed sheets—a random pattern of bright green ferns. A watercolor of a beach scene hangs over the bed and some framed photos are clustered on top of the blond wood dresser. There's not much clutter, because this is Rosie, but she's got the same stuff as regular people, a pile of novels topped by a slightly battered tissue box, a phone charger curling like a clematis vine over the edge of the nightstand.

"I like your sheets," I say as she unzips her jeans and shimmies them off. The effect with her breasts bared sends a fresh surge of blood to my groin.

"Thanks, I just got them. I saw them in a store on Main Street. They reminded me of—" She pauses, her expression growing uncertain.

"Of what?" I ask.

"Your garden."

She seems embarrassed, and I don't want that, so I pull out my secret weapon. I unbutton my shirt and place it on the overstuffed green armchair that makes up the last piece of the room's furniture. Her eyes get big, and I cross over to her, place her hands on my chest. I know she loves it, and I shudder when she strokes my pecs up and down, and then presses her bare breasts against me. We fit together, her supple and pliant, me rigid and ridged.

We sink down onto sheets that are as soft as they look. I pull her over to straddle my lap. With her breasts tantalizingly close to my mouth, I have to taste. While I feast, I unhook her bra. Now she's in nothing but a tiny pair of panties, her loose hair brushing my cheeks as I suckle her. The noises she's making drive me crazy. I have to get inside her.

"Hermosa, I need you."

She moans and kisses me. Her tongue spears into my mouth, wet, hard, fucking hot. I thank the universe that no matter how reserved Rosie can be outside of the bedroom, she doesn't hold back when we're having sex.

She climbs off me, scoots up the bed and watches as I tear off my jeans and boxers, remembering to get a condom out of my pocket first. I toss it on the bed. She kicks off her panties so we're both naked.

"What do you want, Rosie?" I mean tonight, in bed, but there's a part of me that wishes she'd tell me what she wants tomorrow, next week. Forever.

"What do I want?"

"Whatever your heart desires, remember? Your wish is my command. I'll do whatever you want." My tone is serious and my meaning perfectly literal. I would do anything, absolutely anything she asked of me right now. The surge of erotic energy between us at those words is practically palpable.

She feels it too. "Say that again."

"I'll do whatever you want."

"Fuck."

"Including that." I smile a little. "Tell me."

"I want you to come here."

I obey, slotting myself next to her, but I don't touch her. Not yet.

"I want you to make me wet. Well, wetter."

"How?"

"Touch me." She pulls in a ragged breath when I place two fingers over her clit and press gently. "And—and talk to me."

I consider this before I do as she asks. Rosie's not asking for straight-up dirty talk. She's not a prude, but she's not after crude. No, I know her. I know the kind of thing she responds to, but I have to be careful. It will be so easy to go too far, to reveal too much. I can't tell her everything that's growing in my heart, or she'll—honestly, I don't know what she'll do.

But I told her I'd do anything, even this. I place my mouth by her ear, so she can't see my face and she can hide her own if she wants. I keep one hand working the folds of her pussy gently but thoroughly, while the other skims her waist, her tits, the curve of her hip. I keep my voice low and start to talk.

"You're so soft, hermosa. My fingers could sink into you and stroke you forever." She shudders and inches closer. "Would you like that? Let my fingers fuck you and tease you and get you so wet you're dripping, until I finally let you come? I'd keep you here and do it all again, over and over, all night long."

She whimpers and I kiss her shoulder. She smells sweet and tastes salty.

"Soft like a petal, juicy like a fig. Maybe after I make you come with my fingers I'll suck all the nectar off your pussy and drink it down."

Fuck, I want that so bad I have to take a deep breath just to keep from pushing her back on the bed and replacing my fingers with my mouth.

"You taste so good, hermosa—when I'm licking you I can't tell you how hard it makes me to work my tongue right up your soft, wet lips."

I strum her clit like a guitar while she grinds against me, rough and desperate, and I love that she's taking what she wants.

"So soft, so sweet. You make me feel so good, hermosa. You make me want to forget about everything in the entire universe except making you feel good, too." I kiss along the shell of her ear, imagining us as the last two people on earth, existing only for pleasure.

"I want everyone to disappear except us. I'd take you to the meadow, in spring when the sun's warm overhead, the live oaks would shade us. You'd open up like a bud that's finally ready to burst into bloom. I could live there, between your legs, loving— making love to you. Would you let me, Rosie? Let me, please." I'm lost in the fantasy, lost in a haze of need, while she cries out and clenches around my fingers.

She's still moaning and coming but she guides my cock between her legs, pushing aside my hand. I put the condom on one-handed, not wanting to stop touching her even for a second.

I'm only too happy to sink balls-deep in one smooth stroke. She's so wet there's nothing but a slick slide on the way in.

"Fuck. Gus. Yes." I don't know if she's coming again or still coming from before, but she lifts her hips and I start moving, the only sounds our breathing and her broken words as she urges me on. I'm consumed by her smell, by her sounds, by the satin slide of our bodies merging.

She feels so fucking good I can't stop the orgasm that tears through me as I pump into the condom. The pleasure that spirals through me is seemingly endless, until finally I stop. I try not to slump all my weight onto her, but I feel her heart galloping alongside mine as we lie cradled together, still joined as we come down.

"Please." I don't know what I'm saying. I only know that despite having come as hard as I've ever come in my life, I need her, and I'm—scared. I'm scared that I need her more than she needs me. I'm scared that this isn't nearly as important to her as it is to me.

I'm scared I'm in love with someone who's never going to love me back.

"Gus. Hey."

I belatedly realize my eyes have been squeezed shut and I open them with effort. Rosie's looking at me, a little worried.

"Are you okay?"

I don't know if I am, honestly. But none of this is her problem.

"Did you come?" I ask, even though I know she did.

"Yeah." She laughs, runs a hand through her hair, which is looking decidedly post-orgasmic. "Like a hurricane."

"Good."

"You—what you said. It was...beautiful. You're a poet."

I grimace. I don't even know what I was saying. All this intense energy made me a little crazy, maybe.

"Not a poet. Your pussy's just really inspiring." It's not what I mean, what I feel, but I have to put some distance between us or I'm going to say something I'll regret.

"Well, it felt incredible. You did what I wanted." She sounds a little bewildered by that, but it's not like I did anything special. Any sane man would give her anything she wanted and beg her to let them keep giving her everything, forever.

I clean myself up and study Rosie for signs of nerves as she throws on a nightshirt and pair of sleep shorts. But she looks calm and I'm convinced she won't renege on the whole sleep-over thing.

I'm the one who's apparently nervous. I thought I was ready, but now that it's happening, I'm not sure sharing a bed all night is not a terrible idea.

Once I know how it feels to wake up next to her, something tells me it's going to be torture to wake up any other way for the rest of my life.

CHAPTER 24

ROSIE

With Gus in my bed I expect to sleep horribly, but when I pry my eyes open, I've apparently slept the night through unbroken. I turn over and encounter a sleeping Gus. His thick black eyelashes scrape the top of his cheekbones and last night's five o'clock shadow is closer to scruff than stubble. He looks soft and comfy like the threadbare sweater I throw over my pajamas on cool winter mornings.

I ease out of bed as quietly as I can and tiptoe down the stairs to use my downstairs bathroom. The sight of Gus's cowboy boots and my Toms and shirt pooled at the bottom of the stairs reminds me how last night ended up. My nipples harden involuntarily as I remember Gus ravaging them in this very spot the night before.

In the bathroom I splash water on my face, wipe the sleep out of my eyes. The girl looking back at me in the mirror looks rested and happy. Vacation Rosie has great skin.

It's strange, this alternate universe I've been living in for the last couple of weeks. I miss the hospital, miss the routine and the patients and feeling useful. And yet, this time has been precious in other ways. I've slept more, eaten well, read two books. I've helped Nicole with the blasted engagement party. And I've had more sex in the last two weeks than in the last five years.

When I'm back to work, Gus and I won't see each other every day. Maybe he'll want to keep hanging out on the weekends. Maybe he won't. Maybe he'll find someone who can offer him more.

Where do I draw the line? It's getting harder and harder to want to walk away from a guy who says he doesn't want anything long term but who introduces me to his family like it's no big deal. Who likes to spoil me and always puts me first. Who makes me feel beautiful and desirable and feminine and smart. I know I'm all of those things, intellectually. But it's different having someone espouse all your desirable qualities to your face.

But he only knows this version of me—Vacation Rosie, the one who doesn't work twelve-hour shifts and isn't on call on weekends and who doesn't have time for block parties or laying out on the beach. The one who eats takeout and runs on the treadmill instead of making delicious tacos and running on the beach.

The color my life has gained with all my time in the sun these last weeks is just temporary—my real life is spent inside hospital walls, as white and boring as my condo. Dr. Rosie isn't interesting enough for Gus.

He'll figure that out. We'll go back to our separate lives.

I'll be fine.

As usual, I have no food in the house, so we're going to have to go out for breakfast. I make coffee, one thing I never let myself run out of, and take two mugs upstairs. Gus cracks his eyes open and smiles at me, sleepy and satisfied, like a cat. He looks good in my rumpled sheets.

"Coffee?" I hold the mug out toward him.

"In a minute." He stretches and I admire his bare torso. It's not only beautiful, but it represents Gus as a person. Strong, capable, beautiful.

"Tell me about your tattoo," I say impulsively. I've never asked him about the twisted branches that wrap around his right side from his shoulder blade to his abs.

"It's a *Quercus agrifolia*—California live oak tree."

"Why did you get it?"

"Partially to cover up my first tattoo."

"Your first tattoo?" I don't remember seeing another one on him.

"Take a look," he says, twisting around and pointing to his shoulder.

I inspect the dark black ink, leaves and branches, beautifully rendered. The tattoo is large—it must have taken hours. "I don't see anything but the tree."

"There's one leaf that's a little different from the others."

Now that he's pointed it out, I see an oak leaf that's got another type of leaf inside of it in a slightly different color ink.

"A marijuana leaf?" I don't know if laughing is appropriate but I do it anyway.

Gus shakes a rueful head. "I was dumb. Got it on my eighteenth birthday. Thought I was so fly. My mom had a heart attack."

"I'll bet." Mrs. Cuevas doesn't strike me as the kind of mother who would be cool with her teenage son getting a marijuana leaf tattoo.

"When I got the Pacifica Park job I wanted to something to celebrate, so I got a friend to draw this for me." He rolls his shoulders, and the leaves undulate as if blown by the wind. "The live oak is a native tree that thrives in a very specific coastal environment. It's the only oak tree that actually prefers living by the ocean. The cool ocean weather protects it from California's dry spells."

"I know how it feels. I don't think I could live more than five miles from the coast ever again."

"Me either." He smiles at me over this shared preference, as if it bodes well. I don't stop to examine why that makes my belly lurch with nerves. Maybe it's coffee on an empty stomach.

"It's beautiful."

"Thanks."

"Hungry?"

"Yeah." He licks his lips. "Come here."

I laugh and after carefully setting both mugs on my night-stand do as he says. We tumble back into bed together, kissing and touching. It's so, so easy. We know each other by this point, how to touch, how to tease. The intensity of last night's love-making is gone, replaced by something relaxed and familiar that's almost scarier when we orgasm together, Gus pumping deep inside, my name on his lips.

After, I have just enough energy to drag myself back out of bed for the promise of breakfast. I take a lightning fast shower, feeling my blood sugar take a dive. When I emerge from the bathroom, Gus is fully dressed and peering at the pictures on my dresser.

"Is this your brother?" he asks, pointing to the one in the center.

"Yeah. Jake." It's a picture from Jake's high school gradua-tion. I look ridiculously young, my arm around my much taller little brother in his blue cap and gown. Dad's on the other side of Jake, smiling proudly, but there's something about his eyes— they're etched with permanent grief.

"Jake looks like your dad."

"True." I busy myself with pulling out something to wear.

I should elaborate, tell him that Dad died six months after that picture was taken. Heart attack. I was at school sixty miles away, Jake was in a math class at the community college and neither one of us got to say goodbye.

I could tell him that it was almost a relief that he was gone so fast. Dad's soul died when my mother did and even though he hadn't been outwardly ill, it was as if he'd long been suffering from a wasting disease. The heart attack saved him from further years of sorrow.

I say nothing.

"And this is your mom," Gus says as I pull a shirt over my head. "She's beautiful."

I don't have to look to know which picture he means. It's the one of Mom and Jake. Jake's about seven and he's covered in flour. They're rolling out cookie dough to make sugar cookies for my fourth grade class Christmas party. Mom's smiling and she looks young and so pretty.

I remember taking the picture. We didn't have a camera, but I had gotten a disposable camera at a friend's birthday party and I hoarded the photos. That one was special. It made me remember all the good times, all the times Mom took time out of her day to make Jake and me feel special. We didn't have a lot growing up, but I never felt that, not until later. She gave us everything we needed, everything that mattered.

And I couldn't save her.

"Is this one of her, too?" He points to the third and final picture on the dresser. "Is she pregnant with you in this one?"

"I don't really want to talk about it."

"Okay."

I finish getting dressed, silence stretching out painfully between us. Gus gestures to a garment bag hanging over the back of my closet door. "Is that your dress for Nicole's engage-ment party?"

"Uh, yeah."

"Can I see it? Maybe I should try to coordinate."

"What do you mean?" I'm totally lost, feeling that I've missed something crucial while my mind wandered through the painful past.

"I've got a suit, but maybe I should get a new tie. What's this color? I know it has a fancier name than green."

Realization hits me like sudden onset food poisoning. My stomach clenches as if I really might be sick. Gus thinks I'm bringing him to the engagement party. Shit.

CHAPTER 25

ROSIE

"I wasn't planning on going to the party with anyone." I don't mention my pact with the other bridesmaids not to bring dates.

"Oh, sorry. I just—you've been talking about it so much, I guess I thought..." Gus takes in my expression, and frowns. "You don't want me to be there."

"No! It's not that." It's that. "Nicole's going to be stressed, and I'm going to need to be available to her. I'd be a terrible date." That much is true.

"I get it." His mouth thins to a line, and it occurs to me that he probably understands everything I'm not saying. This is why I don't do relationships. I'm awful at them and people get hurt.

"So...breakfast?" I'm such a coward, but I can't think of anything to say that won't make everything worse.

"Rosie, what happens when your vacation is over?"

"What?"

"When you go back to work. What's going to happen?"

I'm not ready to have this conversation. Not on an empty stomach. "Can we talk about this later?"

"There is no later. You're going back to work in a week."

I swallow hard. I've never heard him sound so serious. Why do I feel like crying?

"We said it was a fling," I whisper.

"Yeah. I know what we said." He runs his hands through his hair impatiently. "Rosie, the way I feel about you—it doesn't matter what we thought we wanted. I know what I want now, and it has nothing to do with sex. Well—not *nothing*." He smiles a little and I wish I could smile back. "I think you know that this could be something serious. Something real."

"You don't know what you're saying. You only know Vacation Rosie. I'm not that girl. You don't want the real Rosie."

"Hermosa, you're just you. I know you. I'm falling in love with—"

"No!" The word explodes out of me, desperate to stop him finishing that sentence. I wasn't expecting him to say love. Not after two weeks. Not ever.

"So, I'm good enough to fuck for a couple of weeks but not good enough to date for real?" His eyebrows pull together and I realize how much I'm hurting him, but I can't help it. Dr. Rosie heals her patients and manages to hurt everyone else in her life.

"You deserve more than I could ever give you." It's melodramatic, but true.

"That's bullshit." The anger in his voice makes my head jerk back like I've been slapped.

I've never seen him like this, eyes narrowed hard. Almost as fast as it came over him, the fight goes out and his shoulders slump, his eyes soften along with his voice. "You are everything I want, Rosie. For the first time in my life I'm thinking about the future and I want you in it."

"You don't. You don't know me. You don't know that I don't want to have kids, that my brother barely talks to me. He's engaged and having a baby and I just found out a few days ago that I'm going to be an aunt and the baby's due in a few weeks!"

I don't know why I'm telling him all of this, but maybe if I can get him to see the real me he can leave me and move on. He can find someone else to spoil, someone else to love.

The thought makes me ill.

"Jake avoids me because I remind him of Mom. Our mom, who died because of me."

"What?" His face goes slack. "Didn't you say she died when you were thirteen?"

"Yes."

"How could you possibly…" He shakes his head as if trying to make sense of my madness. "Tell me what happened."

That's the last thing I want to do, but maybe it's for the best. If he knows, then he'll want to leave me anyway.

"She was nine months pregnant. The baby was a surprise, obviously. But she was young, healthy. I was thrilled about getting another sibling. Even Jake was looking forward to it, even though he wouldn't be the baby anymore." I sink down to the floor, unable to support my own weight as I go back to that most horrific of days.

"My dad was at work. He'd taken our only car. We lived way out in the middle of nowhere—orange groves for miles around. The rent was cheap, and Mom adored the scent of orange blossoms." Every spring the air was thick with their perfume.

"Even then, I wanted to be a doctor. Back then it meant dressing up in a smock I pretended was a doctor's coat and looking at people's throats with a Popsicle stick." I had dreams of getting out of our dusty little town and living in a shiny, bustling city.

"That day Mom had gone to her room to take a nap. She'd had a headache and her feet were swollen. She seemed to be sleeping for a long time. I checked on her, and she was white as a sheet. I thought she was still asleep, but her eyes were a little bit open. I knew something was very wrong when she couldn't manage to say anything—she could only moan. Then I saw the blood."

Gus sucks in a noisy breath. I can't look at him.

"She was bleeding, so much. It was a placental abruption, which I didn't know at the time of course. She also had preeclampsia. Between the bleeding and the high blood pressure, she was losing too much blood. I couldn't figure out what to do. I just froze until I realized I needed to call an ambulance. I'd never called 911 before. It seemed like forever before an ambulance actually came. Jake thought the sirens were cool—he didn't understand that Mom was really in trouble.

"The paramedics took Mom out on a gurney. They didn't want to leave us alone, but I told them I'd call my dad."

I wrap my arms around my knees, and Gus sits down on the floor next to me, cradles me against his side. I don't have the strength to reject his comfort, even though I know I don't deserve it.

"She died on the way to the hospital. The baby didn't survive. Too much blood loss."

Gus's voice is rough but clear. "Hermosa, that's not your fault. You called 911. You did everything you could."

"I'd read about preeclampsia in Mom's pregnancy book. I should have checked on her sooner. I should have called the ambulance faster. I should have recognized that when she mentioned the headache, it was something serious. I should have—"

"Stop. You were a child. Not a doctor."

"Jake told me. He said I should have checked on Mom sooner."

"When did he say this?"

"When Dad came home. The paramedics tracked him down at work before I did. He went to the hospital, but she was already dead. They both were. He came home and said, 'Mom's gone.' I didn't understand. I thought he meant from the house, that she was at the hospital. I didn't understand he meant gone, gone. Gone forever."

I've been on the verge of tears for what feels like hours, but my eyes are dry.

"Rosie, God. I'm so, so sorry." He hugs me to him and I let him hold me even as my limbs feel stiff and awkward.

"Now you know why I became a doctor. Why my job is so important to me. Why I can't have a family. Why this is just a fling and why we're...we're over."

The hand stroking my hair falls away.

"Is that really what you want?"

"Yes, of course," I say, but I don't know why I'm saying it. It's what I *should* want. Just like being a doctor. Just like saving people. I *should* do it, so that's what I do.

"Hermosa, you don't have to do this. You don't have to..."

"What?" My eyes burn but the tears still won't fall.

"You don't have to push me away. I'm not asking for—I mean, forget what I said about falling in...well, what I said before. We've only known each other for a little while. I'm just asking you to give us more time."

My voice is toneless when I respond. "That's not possible. I'm going back to the hospital soon. I told you this could only last until I went back to work."

"There are doctors who have lives, you know."

"Not me."

He sighs then, but he doesn't let me go. It occurs to me that he's just as stubborn as I am, that maybe he doesn't buy my workaholic-orphan-girl bullshit.

The thought that he might fight for me fills me with elation and terror. He's the only man I've ever cared enough about to let go of some of my rigidity and actually try. He's the only one who makes me feel like myself, the self I used to be before Mom died and Dad faded away and Jake blamed me for everything. The Rosie who wanted to be a doctor because she thought diseases and broken bones were fascinating, not because she was trying to fix something that could never be fixed.

But if he fights for me, I'll have to make a choice—to fight back, or let him win. I'm a fighter. But the consequences of losing this fight are too dire. I'd lose my heart, and it's been through too much. After this it might never recover.

So I get in the first punch.

"We always had an expiration date, Gus. That hasn't changed. I want to be alone now."

I never said I don't fight dirty.

He doesn't answer right away, but when he does, his voice is full of pain. "If that's what you want."

I hold still, worried if I move the traitorous part of me that's aching to scream *no, stay, love me* will break free.

When I don't say anything, he sighs again. I can't look at his face. I can't believe this hurts as much as it does. How could my dumb idea to have a little vacation fling backfire this spectacularly?

"If you want to, you can call me. Just to talk. Or if you want to try your hand at surfing again. We could be friends."

Why is he being so nice? Why isn't he absorbing the fact that I'm dumping him? He should realize his supply of easy sex is ending and storm out of here.

But he's not that guy. He's one of the good ones. And I'm throwing him away.

"Bye, Gus."

He stands up. I don't watch him go.

"Bye, Rosie."

I don't move until I hear the front door close. I drop my head between my knees. The tears I've been holding back drop hot and angry on the floor between my feet. I've never been more depressed to get what I wanted in my entire life.

CHAPTER 26

GUS

Monday morning continues the stretch of beautiful weather we've been having, but I feel so cold on my drive to work I have to blast the heat. It doesn't really make a difference. Ever since I left Rosie alone yesterday, I've felt vaguely sick. I have to keep reminding myself she'd asked me to leave. I was raised to respect what a woman told me, especially if what she told me was *get the hell away from me*.

But the look on her face when she'd sent me away—she looked *broken*. She'd been broken a long time ago and my asking about her family had brought it all back to the surface.

I wish I'd kept my mouth shut and just let things float along. That's what I usually do and it's kept me out of trouble. The one time I deviate from my MO, it blows up. Hard core.

I itch with the need to know how she is. I want to know that even though she doesn't seem to want anything to do with me, at least she's doing okay otherwise. I could text her, but that might be too pushy. I told her she could reach out to me, but I can't hold my breath waiting for that to happen.

As I pass the main office on my way into work, I realize I have a way to connect. Her friend Nicole's engagement party, the one I'm so pointedly not invited to, is this Saturday. Tessa, Pacifica Park's events coordinator, will have Nicole's contact info. It's not creepy if I ask her to check on Rosie, is it?

Creepy or not, I have to make sure she's okay.

I detour to the office, feeling as out of place as I always do, even though I don't yet have a speck of dirt on me. It's too early for Aradhana or the rest of the office staff, who keep 9-to-5 hours while the garden staff typically work an earlier shift, but I can leave a note for Tessa.

I glance in as I pass Susan's open door and am surprised to see her at her desk. She looks up and calls out to me.

"Gus, what are you doing here?"

I stop in place and hover awkwardly in the doorway. "Just need to leave a note for Tessa about the event this weekend."

"I'm glad you're here, actually."

"Oh?" My palms turn sweaty and I resist the urge to back away.

"Your application package is very impressive. I especially like the ideas you outlined for a water reclamation project."

"Thanks."

"You know, we had thought to open this position up to a nationwide search, but Flora's been insistent that we hire someone in-house. Maybe you knew that already."

"Well, the collection is pretty specialized. Maybe she thinks someone who's already inside will be a better steward of the garden."

"I think you've hit the nail on the head. As far as institutional knowledge goes, you certainly have the edge. No one knows this garden better than you do, except for Flora."

"Thank you." I sense a "but" coming.

"But." There it is. "To be a successful curator you have to have more than just knowledge of the garden. You have to think big picture and long term. We have a multi-year plan and need someone who can implement it. Is that something you think you can do?"

"Is this my interview?" I ask, just to be clear.

Susan shakes her head. "You're right. I'm sorry. We should wait for the formal interview. Okay?"

"Sounds good."

"We have a couple of other internal candidates and the board and I will finish conducting interviews this week. If we don't end up filling the position from those applicants, then we'll open it up to a wider search."

"Understood."

Susan leans forward. "Gus, prepare for that interview, okay? You'll want to put your best foot forward." She looks at me meaningfully.

I nod and continue to Tessa's office, shaking off Susan's implication. She's not trying to be condescending, but it's hard not to take it that way. And she's not wrong. My last job interview basically consisted of Flora asking me what my favorite cycad was, talking plants for two hours, and then her offering me the job. But if I want the directorship, I have to bring more than plant knowledge.

I grab a page from Tessa's sticky note tower, about to scribble my request, when I catch sight of a file on the top of her desk, neatly labeled Winesap-Kendell Engagement Party. I flip it open, jot Nicole's cell number down, and take off. No fuss, no muss.

I'm behind in my rounds due to my detour to the office, so I don't text Nicole till later in the day. I have time to overthink as I'm clearing some debris in the Palmetum. What if I don't get the director job? I might need to see who else is hiring. Maybe I need a fresh start, even if I have to leave Ventura. Starting over somewhere far from Rosie feels completely wrong. But if she's not going to be my future, then I have to be willing to build one somewhere else. With someone else? It's impossible to imagine finding someone I'd want as much as I want her.

Rosie was right. She only allowed me to know a few sides of her. But I love every facet I've seen of complicated, caring, kissable Rosie. I have a feeling if she let me get to know the rest, I'd love each and every one of them, too.

I'm sick with the feeling that I may never get that chance.

GUS

Hi Nicole. This is Gus Cuevas. You might remember me—we met at Pacifica Park a couple of weeks ago when you were there with Rosie. She might have mentioned we've been hanging out. I wanted to ask you to check on Rosie today if you can. We're not seeing each other any more and I'm worried about her. You don't have to text me back if you don't want to. Just check on her. Thanks.

* * *

JESS

So did you man up and ask Rosie to come to Tia Linda's birthday?

GUS

She can't come

You didn't even ask her, did you?

We broke up

Already? You OK?

Not really.

Shit. Do I need to slap someone?

No, nothing like that. Don't worry about it. See you Friday.

OK baby brother. Love you.

Love you too

* * *

NICOLE

How are things?

ROSIE

Fine. How's party planning?

Nightmare. Caterers didn't listen to anything I
told them and Mom just invited 5 more people.
You want to get lunch today?

Don't you have to work?

I can take a lunch break.

I don't know if I can

Meeting up with Gus?

No, that's over

Honey! What happened??

I don't really want to talk about it

Shocker. Lunch. Mandatory. Meet me at the
Ventura Habit.

Fine. But only because I am now craving a
burger.

* * *

ROSIE

Hey girls. I have to tell you something. Even
though Gus was supposed to just be a fling,
things went a little further than that. But we
ended things yesterday. Now Nicole's meeting
me for lunch and I know she's going to try to
get me to get back together with him. Help!

LANI

You got this. Don't let her tell you what to do.
It's your life.

OPHELIA

Try to keep the conversation about the party.
It's this Saturday, so she must be freaking out
about every detail. Distract her.

KATE

Are you OK? Should I come up? What
happened with Gus?

LANI

Yeah, do we need to track Gus down?

> I'm fine. You're sweet, but it's OK. He just
> wanted more than I can give him, I guess.

OPHELIA

They always want more. Smart to end it now.

LANI

Stay strong

KATE

Thinking of you. You know, you can always call
if you want to talk.

> Thanks, ladies. Wish me luck with Nicole.

LANI

She may be the bride, but she's not god.

> I'll try to remember that

CHAPTER 27

ROSIE

Nicole is totally cheating by suggesting lunch at my favorite burger joint. Yes, I love In-N-Out. I am a native Southern Californian, after all. But I maintain that the burgers at The Habit are better. Fight me.

I notice the oil change light comes on when I start up my car. Jake was right, it's time for a service. I might as well take care of it before I go back to work, and I call the dealer to make an appointment on my drive across town.

Nicole and I pull into the tiny parking lot of The Habit near the beach at the same time. Her long blonde hair looks tossed by the perpetual beach breeze. She hugs me, and I hold on a beat longer than I normally do. I just broke up with a boy, am I not allowed an extra-long hug?

"Honey, I'm buying you a burger and you are going to tell me everything."

I think about what the other Never a Brides told me. "I'll tell you what happened, but you have to promise me something: you will not try to fix this."

"But—"

"Nicole. Please. There's nothing to fix."

"Okay, I'll just listen."

I raise my eyebrows.

"And make some minor interjections. And I'll buy you fries."

"And a shake," I grumble.

"Deal."

We order too much food and find a corner table. It's a little late—we must have missed the lunch rush and have the place mostly to ourselves.

I figure Ophelia's distraction advice is worth a try. "How's everything with the party? You said your mom invited more people?"

"Nope, I don't care about the party."

I gasp, truly startled.

"I care about *you*. And so does Gus."

"What?" The lump in my throat makes it hard to speak. Why is my body constantly betraying me? Idiotic lachrymal gland. Stupid parasympathetic nervous system. I hate that I want to cry again.

"He texted me because he's worried about you and wants to make sure you're okay."

"He did?" That *motherfucker*. He left the ball in my court, telling me I could call him, and then he goes behind my back to my best friend to check on me. How dare he?

"I'm going to assume he wouldn't do that if he did the dumping. So tell me what happened."

"Nothing happened. We agreed when we started this that it would be a fling. He got carried away, started thinking about the future. He lied to me. He said he didn't do that, didn't make plans. And then he goes and wants to make plans with me."

"The snake," Nicole says mildly.

"He thought I was going to bring him to the engagement party for some reason. This was only working because I'm on vacation. What kind of girlfriend would I make when I'm at the hospital every day?"

"Probably a challenging one." Nicole's tone holds no judgment.

"Gus doesn't need me in his life. He's got a job he loves and friends and hobbies and he cooks and he's got an adorable nephew and a really cool sister and—"

"You met his sister?"

"And his parents. But it was an accident."

"Of course it was."

"I told him about my mom," I say quietly.

At that, Nicole's gaze turns sharp. "What about her?"

"I told him how she died. What happened to the baby. How I messed up and they died."

Nicole doesn't say anything for a minute and I regret bringing it up. She's the only other person I've ever told what happened. One night in college I was feeling sad and Nicole was trying to get me to come out to yet another party. I snapped and told her exactly why I wasn't in the mood to go out. She tried to make me feel better, murmuring platitudes about how it wasn't my fault and my mom would be so proud of me getting into college all on my own. I appreciated that she cared about me, but she didn't know what she was talking about.

I brace myself for the same vague encouragements: "Oh, honey. I'm so sorry. I messed up. I can't believe this."

"Huh?"

She grabs my hand. Her blue eyes remind me of a cartoon's, wide and unnaturally huge in her face. "Can I ask you something?"

I nod, confused as fuck.

"Have you ever talked to a professional about your mom's death?"

"What, like a therapist? No." I swallow nervously. Jake's revelation that he's been going to therapy has definitely been on my mind ever since, but having Nicole bring it up too is a bit much.

"So your mom dies tragically when you're thirteen and you never think maybe you should get some therapy about it? You're a doctor. Therapy's good for you."

"I know therapy can be helpful. I just never thought I needed it." Therapy's for other people. People who don't know what's wrong with them. People who deserve to get better.

"You're a thirty-year-old woman who's never had a serious relationship. You're a workaholic commitment-phobe. You didn't last more than two weeks with the only guy I've ever seen you really care about. I love you, and you need therapy, honey."

"Wow." I pull my hand away, because that's a lot to take in.

"I totally screwed up because I knew you were blaming yourself way back in college. But I thought that you'd forgiven yourself, that you'd grown up. You always did so well in school and you were always so focused, so driven. I assumed that meant you were happy. I should have made sure, I should have pushed."

The idea of Nicole pushing harder makes me shudder.

"Nicole, you're not responsible for me."

"I was there when your father died. You didn't even have a funeral because there wouldn't have been anybody there. I *am* your family. Kate's your family. Ophelia. Maybe Gus, too. Even if you guys aren't meant to be together romantically, he could be your friend."

The buzzer indicating our meal is ready goes off and I jump at the noise. Nicole sighs, scoops up the buzzer and goes to the counter to collect our food. I take a minute to absorb what she's telling me.

Finally, I get it. I'm not Nicole's responsibility, but she's taking me on anyway.

There I go, wanting to cry again.

"Here," she says, thrusting a stack of napkins in my face. "Go ahead."

I smile at her, eyes watery. "Nicole, you are such a pushy bitch. But I love you."

I'm sure she realizes I've never said that to her before. The love part, I mean. The force of her smile knocks me back a little. "I know you do, honey."

"Okay. So I'll go to therapy. Jake said that his fiancée is making him go, too. I guess the Snyder siblings are more messed up than I realized."

"Wait, Jake's got a fiancée?" Nicole steals one of my fries. She didn't order any of her own, naturally.

"Apparently. I just found out about her. They're expecting a baby." I take a deep breath. The idea of my brother becoming a father is starting to sink in. I'm happy and sad simultaneously. I guess that's normal. That's life. That's love. And soon, when he's married and has a child, I'll have more people in my life to love.

"That's fantastic! Good for Jake."

"Yeah. He's not a kid anymore."

She sighs theatrically. "None of us are. Now, tell me about Gus."

"I did. It's over."

"No, all you said was that you told him about your mom. Then what?"

My mind shies away from remembering yesterday's awful scene, but if things are going to get better, I'll have to get better at examining things I don't really want to.

"He...he held me. He told me he was sorry about Mom. He asked me to give us more time." Saying it out loud makes me realize how little he'd actually asked for at all.

"And you said...?" Nicole prompts me when I fall silent.

"I said he deserved more than I could give him and he didn't know the real Rosie, just Vacation Rosie, and that I wanted to be alone."

"Ouch."

"I think I was scared if I gave him more time and he found

out that Real Rosie wasn't someone he wanted to be with, it would hurt more in the long run than if I just ended it."

"Stop it with this Real Rosie/Vacation Rosie nonsense." She points at me. "This is the real you. You've got issues, whether or not you're working. But you're also fun, you're sweet, you care about helping people. It doesn't matter if you're a doctor or a teacher or a CEO. You'd still be *you*. Gus clearly likes *you*. The question is, do *you* like *Gus*? I only met him for two seconds. What's he like?"

I struggle to put everything I feel about Gus into words. "He's...a regular guy. And an extraordinary man. He knows the name of every plant ever, and its history and what makes it special. He likes local beer and grilled meat and he's always wearing some kind of hat, even though he has the most gorgeous hair. He loves his family, though they don't understand him. He's the only guy I've ever slept with who actually makes me come in the missionary position." I clasp my hand over my mouth after that last one, then shrug. "Sorry. TMI."

She waves away my apology. "No such thing, honey. So, he's good in bed?"

"Kind of insanely good."

"I can see why you decided on a fling. Three weeks of great sex—not the worst plan ever. I guess he wasn't boyfriend material, though?"

"He'd make a great boyfriend, just not for me. He can cook. He knows all these out-of-the-way restaurants that I've never heard of but where the food is amazing. He tried to teach me to surf. He knows everyone on the Avenue. He's just...a really great guy."

"Hmmm." Nicole pushes aside her half-eaten hamburger. "Honey, you're a medical doctor, but I'm a love doctor. You've got a terminal case. Official diagnosis: you're in love."

"You're crazy. Where did you get your degree? You've been with one guy your entire life."

"False. I've been with Ricky for eight years, but I had plenty of experience before he took me off the market."

It's true. Nicole was willing to try anything once, maybe twice, until Ricky convinced her to be a one-man girl junior year of college.

"I know what I'm talking about. Gus is sweet and good in bed. He's got a job, his own place, and a relationship with his family. He also gets you. Two more things: you asked him to leave, and he left. He respected your wishes. But he was worried enough about you to get in touch with me."

"Yeah. I guess that's kind of unusual." I'm exceedingly grumpy about having to acknowledge that Nicole may have a valid point.

"I've heard enough horror stories about the current dating scene to know this guy is a catch."

"Nicole, you promised you wouldn't try to fix this."

"I'm not fixing it. That's what you're going to have to do."

I'm back to thinking of her as a pushy bitch, but relent a little.

"I'll think about the therapy. I'll try to calm down about work. Maybe even think about dating more regularly. But Gus. I care enough about him to know that he should be with someone else. Someone better for him."

She doesn't look entirely happy but in the end she says, "Okay, I promised and I'll leave it at that. Thanks for thinking about therapy."

"Thanks for lunch." I hope she knows I mean thanks for everything. "Now, tell me about the problem with the caterers."

ROSIE'S STAYCATION TO DO LIST

- ~~beach day~~
- ~~bookstore~~
- ~~go to the movies~~
- museum?
- ~~get pedicure~~
- laundry — wash sheets?
- learn to cook
- look up recipes online
- grocery shopping
- get therapist
- oil change
- learn how to be normal
- Jake and Becca baby/engagement/wedding present
- another pedicure?

GUS

I sit in the reception area outside of Susan's office and resist the urge to run. This situation embodies everything I hate about traditional jobs. I'm wearing slacks, not work pants, and a shirt with buttons, tucked in no less. I traded my work boots for clean black sneakers. I gelled my hair. I miss my hat.

The longer I sit in the narrow hallway, the more my pulse races. I have flashbacks sitting in school, bored out of my mind, walls closing in on me.

Why am I even putting myself through this nonsense? I could be outside, my fingers in the dirt, the sun on my back. I could be working, doing my job, not pretending to be someone I'm not.

When I have to go into that room I'll be pretending to be someone who can straddle both worlds. I have to act like I can sit in meetings and planning sessions and reach a consensus and think about things like budgets and schedules. Who am I kidding? I should stick to what I know, what I'm good at.

I couldn't hold onto Rosie. I don't have it in me to make it at this, either.

Across from my seat there's a lithograph on the wall, an

early print of the garden when Esme Archer first opened it to the public. The palm garden is there, recognizable even back then. It's a unique collection, but we could be doing so much more. I straighten my back.

No one knows this garden like me, not even Michelle with her stuck-in-amber attitude. The garden must evolve. I can lead the effort. I found a life here. I want to give back and leave my mark on it. Flora's leaving a legacy of hard-fought changes and I can help preserve that legacy and go even further.

I jump when the door opens to let in a docent and three older women in matching pink baseball caps and floral print shirts. I smile at the docent, Lottie. She's been here as long as I have, and she gives me a hug.

"Ladies, this is a treat, you're getting to meet one of the most important people at Pacifica Park. This is Gus. He's responsible for the Palmetum, among other things around here."

The women coo and start talking over each other about how much they love the Palmetum.

"Marilyn here had a question about the Pondoland palm, and why it's so special. Maybe you can tell us, Gus," Lottie says.

"That's very astute, Marilyn." The cheeks of the woman next to Lottie pink up. "Actually, species like the Pondoland palm are why our conservation efforts at Pacifica Park are so vital. This palm, native to South Africa, is nearly extinct in the wild, and we've had difficulty getting our seeds to germinate. We have a campaign right now to expand our conservation efforts. I hope you'll consider donating before you leave."

There's much assurance that they will, and Lottie gives me a wink as they walk through toward the gift shop. "I'll make sure they pony up before they go."

"Nicely done."

I swing around in the direction of the offices and see Susan standing with her arms crossed and an impressed look on her face. "Education and advocacy, with a little flattery to boot."

I smile. "Talking about plants is easy for me."

"I knew you were an expert, but I didn't realize how passionate you are about this garden's efforts in particular."

She gestures to the room behind her, where the interview committee sits in conference. "Listen, the board members in there are more worried about whether we can make our fundraising goals and grow our endowment than about the Pondoland palm. But I care that we're fighting to preserve as many species as possible. So I want you to go in there and stun them with your fiscal responsibility and let me worry about the rest."

I straighten my shoulders. I'm not afraid anymore. I want this job. I'm the best person for it, and I'm going to get it. I follow her into her office where three middle-aged white guys in suits are waiting with expectant faces.

I nail it.

* * *

Later that day, when Susan tells me I got the job, the first person I want to call is the last person who wants to hear from me.

I sigh. Pacifica Park is my home. It's where I'm going to make my mark. I was afraid of reaching too high and failing. But I haven't been giving myself enough credit for what I've already accomplished. Rosie might not want to be a part of my future, but it feels like a victory to even be thinking about what I want for myself next year, or five years from now. I'm ready to stop living for today and start planning for tomorrow. I'm ready to start building on the foundation I didn't realize I've been laying out, one plant at a time.

I open my phone, go to my texts. My finger hovers over Rosie's name. I glance at the last text we exchanged. Me, confirming our dinner Saturday night. Her simple affirmation.

I'm such an idiot. She told me she wanted a fling. She told me she didn't have time for a boyfriend. She told me she wasn't looking for anything serious. She never lied to me. Why was it so shocking that when I pushed for more, she pushed me away? I should have expected it. I shouldn't have pushed.

I sigh heavily. I have to trust that Nicole's going to look out for her, since I can't.

I have to let her go.

CHAPTER 29

ROSIE

The car dealership where Jake works is a shiny, modern beehive, a large gray building surrounded by row after row of gleaming cars. I'm hot and sticky since it's easily ninety degrees. Southern California weather is tricky. October comes and you think you may be in for a break from the relentless summer heat, but somehow it only gets hotter and drier. Today is hot, bright, sunny. The opposite of my mood.

I pull up to the service side of the complex, hand my keys to the attendant, then go into the main building to get processed. The inside is cool and dim, and it takes a second for my eyes to adjust. A young woman with a visible baby bump waves me over to her cubicle.

I barely have time to notice her nametag reads Becca before she leaps out from behind her keyboard to wrap me in a hug. "It's you!" she squeals. "OMG, Jake didn't tell me you were coming by. I'm so excited!"

It wouldn't take someone with a medical doctorate to figure out that this is Jake's Becca, his fiancée and mother of his future child.

"Hi," I say weakly and completely inadequately in the face of Becca's zeal.

She laughs. "I'm Becca."

"I got that." I try to make my smile warm. "I'm Rosie, but I guess you figured that out."

"Rosie, I've been bugging Jake to meet you for ages. But you know how he is—he didn't even tell me he loved me until we'd been dating a whole *year!*"

"That sounds about right."

"He's had a tough time, well, you know. But when does talk about it, he always tells me how amazing you were and how you basically raised him and made sure he had everything he needed. You're the best big sister ever! I hope someday if this little baby girl becomes a big sister, she'll be as awesome as you are."

I'm speechless. Jake said I was amazing? Maybe she's dating some other Jake Snyder.

It's all too much to process, so instead of trying, I pounce on the one detail I can wrap my head around. "You're having a girl?"

"Yes! OMG, Jake didn't tell you? Of course he didn't. Yes, we're having a girl."

"That's wonderful." I inject as much enthusiasm into my voice as I can, but it still pales in comparison to Becca's apparent unbridled joy at life.

"Let me get you processed." She takes my paperwork and calls me up on the computer.

"So, you and Jake met here?" Knowing my brother, I'll be lucky to be invited to the wedding, so this may be my only chance to interrogate my future sister-in-law.

"We worked together for six months before I'd dropped enough hints that he finally asked me out." Becca grins as if my brother's shyness is the most adorable thing in the world.

"You're from the area?"

"Born and raised in Santa Barbara. Went to UCSB for finance. I'm actually the chief loan officer here, but we're short-staffed today so I'm pitching in with the service department."

I'm not surprised, but I am impressed. "Jake told me you were smart."

She beams. "He just worships the ground you walk on," she says. "He'd want to impress you, being a doctor and everything. Sign here and initial here." She points to a printout and I scribble my signature.

Jake worships the ground I walk on? That can't be right. "Well, I'm so happy to meet you."

"Wait, let me take my coffee break and we can talk more!"

My face might fall off from all the polite smiling I'm doing, but I can't deny her and we settle into the waiting area with cups of complimentary coffee—decaf for Becca. She sighs, tucking her feet underneath her and rubbing her beach-ball shaped belly.

"How's everything going?" I ask, channeling my doctor persona. "You feeling good?"

"I feel fantastic. Well, I do now, anyway. The first trimester I couldn't keep a thing down, but as soon as I hit twelve weeks, I started to feel sooo much better."

"That's great. And you don't have high blood pressure or any family history of complications?"

She laughs. "I'm healthy as a horse. Honestly, we thought it would take longer to get pregnant, which is why we're doing things a little bit backward with the wedding and everything, but apparently I'm really fertile so we got lucky, so to speak, on the first try."

The fact that this pregnancy was planned is a bit of a surprise. I assumed Jake wouldn't want kids, like me. But it seems I've been wrong about most of my assumptions when it comes to my brother. "Congratulations. I'm really happy for you two."

"Thanks! You have to be at the wedding, of course. We're not doing anything super fancy. We're saving for a house, so there's really no point. I'm kind of super cheap. My cousin just got engaged and you would not believe the amount of money they are spending on the wedding. Their engagement party alone is a fancy dress thing where they reserved an entire garden."

"What? Who's your cousin?"

"Ricky Kendell—why, do you know him?"

This is too weird. "He's marrying my best friend."

"You're friends with Nicole?" Becca's excitement doubles and I worry a little for her blood pressure.

"I'm one of her bridesmaids."

"That is unbelievably cool!"

"Are you going to the engagement party?"

"My mom's making us." She wrinkles her nose. "No offense, I love Ricky, but I'm not exactly thrilled about squeezing into something fancy-garden-party appropriate. Not to mention shoes! The only pair that fit me right now are my bedroom slippers."

I laugh. "I feel you. I hate shopping."

"What are you wearing?"

I tell her about the dress Nicole made me buy and we talk about clothes, and the engagement party, and how her mom, Ricky's mom's sister, doesn't understand why her daughter works at a Japanese car dealership. "You could at least work for Mercedes, darling." Becca's imitation of her mother's drawl makes me laugh.

We're still laughing when Becca glances at her phone screen. "Shoot, I've got to get back to work." She stands up just as a tall man in a gray mechanic's jumpsuit enters the waiting area. "Jake, hey, baby." Becca gives Jake a hug, and he hugs her back easily. Apparently the Snyders are huggers now.

"So you guys met," Jake says. He seems relaxed and happier than I've seen him in a long time.

"Yeah, no thanks to you," Becca says, but there's no heat in her words. She seems to legitimately love my taciturn, emotionally constipated brother.

Suddenly my chest tightens with pride. He's thriving, and if what Becca's said is true, I had something to do with that.

"Your car is ready," he says to me. "I changed the air filter and next time you're probably going to need to do your brakes. But otherwise it's in great shape."

"Thanks, Jake." I smile at him, hoping some of the love and pride that's currently swamping my chest cavity shows in my eyes.

He smiles back and I think maybe he understands. "No problem, Ro."

Ro. He hasn't used the nickname in years. I smile harder.

"So, we'll see you Saturday," Becca says brightly.

Jake looks confused and Becca elaborates. "Ricky's fiancée is Rosie's best friend."

"Seriously?" Jake's met Nicole a few times over the years, but he must not have put two and two together.

"We're going to be family," Becca proclaims.

"Family," I echo. For the first time, I really accept the idea that Mom's death doesn't have to mean that Jake and I are doomed to be alone. One thing I've learned from my job is if you have people willing to show up at your hospital bed when you really need them, you're doing something right.

Why have I been hell-bent on keeping Gus on the outside, when letting him in would feel so much better?

CHAPTER 30

GUS

Friday after work I stop by the nursery to pick out a special plant for Tia Linda. My favorite aunt loves red, so I select a brightly hued bougainvillea in a three-gallon pot. I'll plant it by her back gate where it can take over and provide endless blooms.

I don't exactly want to spend the entire evening surrounded by my family, but I haven't seen them in a while and it might be nice. It'll get my mind off Rosie, anyway. As much as I've tried to stop thinking about her, I find myself constantly wondering what she's doing, how she's feeling. Hoping she's not being too hard on herself.

It's a bit of a hike inland to Santa Paula where Tia Linda lives a few streets over from where Jess and I grew up, but it's worth it to see her light up over the bougainvillea.

"Your mama's in the kitchen and your papa's running the little kids ragged around the yard."

"I'll find them after I plant this for you," I say, holding it up. "Remember—you gotta water it until it establishes itself, okay?"

"I won't forget," she promises.

I head to the back, waving at various cousins and family

friends on my way. I find a shovel and gloves in Linda's back shed and dodge screaming five-year-olds as I walk to the rear property line. I helped Linda plant the shade trees that line the sturdy wooden fence a few years ago, and am pleased to see their steady growth, providing her with shade and privacy from her neighbors. It's nice to see the hard work we put in a long time ago paying off. There's a bare spot along the back that the bougainvillea will fill in nicely.

I judge the spot I want to dig, taking into consideration the sun, drainage, the likely growth pattern after the vine establishes itself. I don't want it to overtake her gate. I grab the shovel and get to work. It's quick work to dig the proper sized hole. I grab the garden hose, the metallic scent of the water as it comes flowing out taking me back to childhood, trailing my dad around our tiny postage-stamp sized lawn as he watered the thorny shrub roses and always near-death grass.

"Hello, son." My dad comes up to me just as I'm sliding the plant into its new home and start filling in with soil. "What are you doing?"

I try to refrain from saying something smart-mouthed. "Tia Linda's birthday present," I say instead. "Flame-colored bougainvillea."

"Thoughtful of you," he says, surprising me. He glances around the yard. The light is dimming, and most of the guests have gathered on the back patio, crowding around the grill. I spot my mother putting a casserole on a big folding table, and Jess and Carla trying to herd the kids toward the picnic table that's been set up just for them.

"I remember when you planted these trees. They look good."

"Thanks. You and mom should let me work on your yard." I've offered a million times and they always put me off.

"We rent. What's the point?"

"I rent. The point is what do you want to look at every day? Dead grass?"

"Don't worry about us," he says.

Some long-tamped down frustration rises to the surface and I burst out with words I didn't know were on the tip of my tongue. "What I do—it's important."

His eyebrows lift at my tone.

"Making things grow. Making things beautiful. I know it's not what you and Mom wanted for me. But it's what I want."

The eyebrows drop and his voice sounds a little sad. "I know that, son."

"Well, I want to show you. I'm picking you up tomorrow morning and we're going to my garden. I want you to see it properly. Because I'm going to be there for a long time. I just got promoted. Director of horticulture. More money. More responsibility. More say in the future of the garden."

My father is silent for a moment, as if he's struggling for words. I wonder how my parents could have been so fucking chill when Jess announced that she was a lesbian, had no problem reconciling their conservative upbringing with Jess's life, welcomed Carla and her son with open arms, and have such trouble with me being a goddamned gardener. I'm about to burst out with my anger, when he finally speaks.

"I'm proud of you, Gustavo."

My anger floats away like dandelion seeds on the wind. "You are?" I can't help the disbelief in my voice.

"Of course," he says brusquely. Then he swallows and speaks again, not quite meeting my eyes. "You've become a fine man. I didn't always know the best way to reach you when you were younger. I was afraid if I pushed you too much in one direction, you'd go the opposite. But you found your way, even if I wasn't there to guide you."

It's the tone of his voice that makes my own voice thick when I respond. "Thanks, Dad."

We don't go so far as to hug, but standing there in the fading sunlight, dirt under my fingernails, and my dad standing by my side, I realize I don't need the hug. I don't even really need the approval. I just need my family. And they're right here with me.

Later, when the mountains of food have been properly decimated, my dad surprises me by announcing to everyone that I've been promoted, and I get a round of applause and hooting and hollering. Jess is beaming and Carla gives me a high five. "Way to go, Gus."

My mom looks reluctant to join in, but when she sees that everyone else thinks this is a good thing, she smiles, too, sucking up the attention by proxy. I tell her she's coming to the garden tomorrow and I won't take no for an answer.

"I should have insisted you come years ago. You're going to love it, I promise."

"All right, Gus." She pats my arm. "Will you bring Rosie with you so I have someone to talk to?"

I freeze. I forgot that she's met Rosie. That she might ask about her.

"No, Rosie—" I look around helplessly. *Doesn't love me. Doesn't want to be with me.* "—can't be there."

"Too bad. I like that girl. So pretty. And a doctor, too!"

"Yes, Mom, we all know that she's a doctor, and she's way out of my league. You don't have to rub it in." I admit I sound slightly pathetic.

Mom looks surprised. "Out of your league? I think you make a nice couple, but she's the lucky one. Look at my son, handsome, smart, takes good care of his parents and his sister and his tias and primos. And now a promotion! She's the lucky one."

I stare at my mother in shock. What is this, parental approval night? I can't bring myself to tell her that Rosie doesn't want anything to do with me. I wish she was here so I could introduce her to the people I love, the people who've known me all my life. I wish I could show her off and hold her hand and steal kisses and feed her Tia Linda's famous tres leches cake. I wish she'd seen me as worth taking a chance on. I rub my chest, as if I can make the hurt go away like a muscle cramp.

"Thanks, Mom."

"Well, bring her for dinner sometime."

I pause. "I hope to." It's not a lie.

Maybe I'll never stop hoping where Rosie's concerned.

CHAPTER 31
GUS

"And this is the Palmetum, where I spend most of my time." I gesture to the unusually blue *Brahea armata* and the hundred-year-old Chilean wine palm. "Though I'm also responsible for the other palms in the garden, like the ones lining the main drive."

"I found a seed!" Eddie picks up a pea-sized red seed and shows it off proudly.

"That's right. That's from a King palm. It's naturally found in Australia and on islands in that region. See how it's different from this one?" I hold up a two-inch-long date.

Jess and Carla are walking around, soaking up the sunshine, while Eddie has to stop and touch everything. I make a mental note to avoid the cactus garden until he's a little older.

Dad stops by a cluster of small palms, feathery fronds coming off slender stalks. "These are beautiful. They remind me of Huatulco," he says, naming a city where a few of our cousins live.

"That's because they're from Oaxaca. Most *Chamaedorea* are from Central America."

"Really?" Dad looks pleased to have recognized them.

Mom has been unusually silent during the entire tour. She

looked surprised when I showed her the main office, with its opulent tile work and fancy gift shop. She smiled when I introduced her to Tessa, who's running around like a maniac to get ready for Nicole's engagement party. And when Susan unexpectedly popped her head out of the office while we were in the gift shop and said, "We're so lucky to have Gus and I'm excited to be working more closely with him on the future of the park," all Mom could manage to say was, "Thank you."

Now she's staring at a *Butia capitata*. I stand next to her, more than a head taller in my work boots.

"Thanks for coming, Mom." It doesn't matter if she still doesn't get what I do. It matters that she's letting me try to share it with her.

"Everything is so...beautiful." She puts her arm around my waist, squeezes. "I had no idea. I guess I didn't try to understand."

I hug her back. It's more than I ever thought I'd get from her.

We wander by the cannas and the succulents and pause when we reach the lawn. Workers in uniforms are running around setting up tables and a dance floor and arranging chairs. Tessa's in the middle, directing traffic and talking into her smartphone at the same time.

"What's going on?" Mom asks.

"Special event. We have all kinds. Tonight's an engagement party."

"Do they do weddings, too?"

"Sure." I cut my eyes to her, suddenly suspicious. "Why?"

She grins. "No reason. Just thinking ahead."

I don't take the bait and instead turn my back on the party preparations. I don't need to be imagining Rosie there later tonight, looking beautiful in her fancy green dress. She's a bridesmaid, and there will probably be groomsmen there, more than likely Santa Barbara bros who know a good thing when they see it. They'll ask her to dance and she'll be awkward at first and eventually accept and—it hits me that I don't know if Rosie's a good dancer. I don't know what it feels like to hold her and move to music. I feel robbed that I won't get the chance to find these things out for myself.

I tear myself from this line of thought. "Who's hungry for lunch? We can go to The Spot for burgers."

"Yeah!" Eddie yells and runs ahead and I laugh. See, life goes on after your heart gets broken. I just need more time.

I glimpse a familiar blonde head striding across the lawn, arms full of an enormous cardboard box. I jog over, momentarily abandoning my family.

"Nicole, hey, it's Gus." We only crossed paths briefly the first time I met Rosie, but I remember everything about that day with crystal clarity.

"Gus?" Nicole can barely see me over the box. "Little help?"

I take the box from her. It's not heavy, just big and awkward. "What's all this?"

"Party favors."

I glance inside and see dozens of what look like seed packets made from beautiful handmade paper.

"Did you make these?"

"I designed them, yes. Made the prototype and got some of my crew to assemble them. They're seed packets, with seeds in the paper so you can plant the packaging, too."

"Genius," I say. They're beautiful, functional, unique, creative, and make the world prettier. I approve. Miles better than the usual plastic shit that'll end up in a landfill.

"Thanks. You working today?"

"No, giving my family a tour." I indicate the group behind me, flush a little when I realize they're all nakedly staring at my interaction with the pretty blonde girl. "I hope everything goes great tonight," I say, meaning it. I have to bite my tongue so I don't ask about Rosie. I'm dying to, but I'm acutely aware it's not my place.

"Thanks, I think it's going to be a night to remember." She tucks a strand of hair behind her ear.

I fidget, her stare unnerving. Is there a bee on my nose? "What?"

"I think you should come."

"Excuse me?"

"To the engagement party. I would absolutely love it if you could make it. You have a suit, right?"

"Yeah, but—"

"Most of the people coming are my parents' friends. Ricky and I only moved back a little while ago so we're woefully lacking in friends our own age and you'd be doing me a huge favor. You can meet the other bridesmaids and the food is going to be awesome. Please, please tell me you can make it."

I stare at her. This is undoubtedly a girl used to getting her own way 100 percent of the time. But she's so genuine in her manipulation that you kind of admire her for it.

"You know that Rosie isn't going to want to see me, right?"

"All I know is that she's coming solo. Actually, all my bridesmaids are, for some reason." She frowns briefly, then the sunny smile resumes. "Besides, I'm not inviting you because of Rosie. I'm inviting you because I like you and I want you there."

I furrow my brow, feeling stubborn. "If you like me so much, what's my last name?"

"Cuevas, Gus, short for Gustavo, named after your father. Is that Gustavo Senior up there? I see good looks run in the family." She actually finger waves in the direction of my parents. "Is that your mom? Maybe I should go introduce myself and—"

"Okay, okay, I'll come." Jesus, my palms are sweating. "You are devious."

She laughs, a tinkly sound that's somehow threatening. "I love Rosie. She's been through a lot and she has a lot to work out. I think you're good for her. But if I suspect for a minute that you are going to hurt her, I won't hesitate to step in and make it impossible for you to hurt anyone because you'll be in too much pain to move. Got it?"

I shiver involuntarily. "Got it. What time tonight?"

"Seven. Formal dress. No gifts."

CHAPTER 32

ROSIE

I don't need my GPS to get to the garden anymore. Even in the near dark, I drive the twisty, narrow road with ease. The familiar big metal gates stand open, lit by lamps giving it the aura of the old-timey estate it once was.

I park and check my lipstick one last time in the rearview mirror. I look okay in the dress that Nicole picked out for me. I've got on new earrings, too, green enamel ferns I bought at a shop on Main Street. They reminded me of Gus the minute I saw them.

I owe it to Nicole to look my best and try to have fun. At least the other Never a Brides won't have dates, either. We'll stick together and snark about the other guests.

Still, I'm not much in the partying mood. I can't seem to go a few seconds without thinking about how wrong I was, about everything from thinking my brother blamed me for Mom's death, for how long I've spent blaming myself, and most of all, for believing Gus and I could never be more than a fling.

Because Nicole was right. I'm in love with Gustavo Cuevas.

I'd like to believe that he'd give me another chance. As scary as it would be to put my heart out there, risking it being smashed to smithereens, I know it would be safe with Gus. He's not the kind of guy who smashes things. He nurtures them. He waters and feeds and cultivates. Being with him is like getting a dose of sunlight and organic fertilizer for my soul.

Together we could build something new. For the first time, I can honestly say I don't want my life to be defined by loss, but by growth.

Where better to grow than in a garden?

I'll come back here again someday and I'll ask him for the same thing I couldn't bear to give him—time.

Charming signs studded with glittering stars direct me from the parking lot to the big lawn for a night of "Starry Romance." I set aside my hopes, my plans, and steel myself for the night ahead, pasting a smile onto my face.

The catering staff, the DJ, and Tessa, whom I remember from my first visit to the garden, are all in place, looking competent and busy. The stage is set—all that's needed are the actors to begin the play. Strings of artfully placed globe lights make the garden glow. The breeze stirs the fronds of the palms that rise all around, making a shushing sound like the ocean at low tide. We're in a magical fairyland of our own making.

I'm hit with a wave of homesickness so strong I nearly stumble in the grass. But what am I homesick for? Not my boring, bare apartment. Not the hospital, antiseptic and fluorescent. Not my family, the way it was so long ago I can barely remember. I have a new family now, and it's growing by the second.

Maybe I'm homesick for something I haven't experienced yet. A place that's warm and full of love, full of hope. I'll feather my nest with hope for the future, instead of sadness about the past.

I step onto the hard floor that's been installed for tonight, and it feels like stepping into that future. I glance around. I'm the only one here. That's okay. I'm strong enough to face my future alone.

But then Nicole appears, holding Ricky's hand. She looks like a princess in a silver dress composed of a tight bodice and a flowing, floor-length skirt. Ricky stands dapper and decorous in a black suit, crisp white shirt, and black tie. They're smiling at me. My eyes prick with tears.

Right behind them come Ophelia, Lani, and Kate, all in shades of green, like me. They walk close together, heads bent toward each other, and Lani says something to make the other two laugh. I smile reflexively, certain I'd be laughing if I'd heard the joke, too.

"Hey, Sis." I turn around and Jake's there, tall and lanky, his arm around Becca, perfectly adorable in a simple black dress and pearls, cradling her baby bump as if she's a modern-day Madonna.

I give them each a hug. "You clean up nice, baby brother," I say, because if I don't tease him I'll break down and blubber over how handsome he is.

"You too, Ro," he says. More guests start to arrive, but Nicole and Ricky ignore them in favor of coming to greet Jake, Becca, and me.

"Hey Becca," Ricky says, and Nicole swivels her head back and forth between her fiancé, my brother, and Becca so fast I'm worried she'll pull a muscle. I totally forgot to tell her the connection.

"What's going on here?" she asks, as if she's the victim of some big conspiracy.

"You've met my cousin, Becca," Ricky says.

"Of course. It's great to see you again," Nicole says politely.

"And you've met my brother, Jake," I say.

"It's been a while, but yes."

"Well, Becca and Jake are engaged," I continue.

"With a baby on the way," Becca throws in perkily.

"Which means…" I prompt.

Nicole's eyes widen. "Oh my fucking God!"

I can't help the laughter that bubbles out of me at Nicole's exclamation. She hardly ever swears, so when she does, it's an event.

"We're going to be related, Rosie. Oh my God." She clutches my arm.

"Are you crying? Don't cry, sweetie," I say, petting her hair, wishing I'd thought to bring tissues in my impractically tiny clutch.

"But we're, I mean, I know two couples have to get married to make this official—but we will literally be related!"

I was kind of blown away by the coincidence involved, but seeing Nicole's emotional reaction has me realizing the enormity of it. I've gone from having just my brother to having one of my best friends become family in a matter of days.

"You're already my sister," I say, because she's the one who's always brave and says things like that. I want to be brave, too. "And now you're going to be my cousin, too."

"Stop!" Nicole presses her fingers to the bottom of her eyes to try to stop the tears.

Ricky fishes a handkerchief out of his pocket, because he's the kind of guy who carries a handkerchief. Nicole takes it gratefully.

"Welcome to the family, Jake, Rosie." Even though the general consensus is that Ricky is boring as dirt, I suppose there's something to be said for being reliable enough to be considered boring. He's always there for Nicole, and that says a lot.

I smile at him and Jake says a gruff, "Thanks, man." He seems happy. It must have been hard on him, too, having no one but a workaholic sister who lived far away for most of the last decade. He's probably a little nervous to become a dad, but to have Ricky consider him a part of their family now, that's huge. It's a relief to know that even if something happened to me, Jake won't be left alone. He'll have Becca and Ricky and Nicole and the little baby presently in Becca's belly.

I'll have them, too.

I'm strong enough to face my future alone, but I'm glad I don't have to. The Never a Brides don't need boyfriends to make our lives complete, but that doesn't mean we don't need anyone at all.

CHAPTER 33

GUS

The garden is different at night. The familiar plants and well-worn paths transform into abstract shapes and dark lanes in the darkness.

It's unsettling to feel so out of place in my second home, but maybe it's just my outfit: dark gray suit, crisp white shirt, skinny black tie. Everything bought for Jess and Carla's wedding and hardly worn since. Gravel digs through the thin soles of my dress shoes. I might as well be barefoot. I feel almost naked out of my normal work clothes, the boots and pants and gloves that protect me on the job.

I need a different sort of armor tonight.

Even though Nicole swears she invited me here for her own reasons, I think we both know that I'm here to see Rosie. Staying away from her this last week has been torture. Not knowing if she's okay, regretting that I ever agreed to the stupid fling in the first place. Wishing I'd had the foresight to realize that this girl was special, that she was worth waiting for.

Night in the garden. Familiar yet foreign. Too many shadows. Too easy to get lost in the dark maze of my thoughts.

The party seems to be in full swing by the time I finally reach the lawn. It's pretty much what I expected: a bunch of white guys in black suits, the women on their arms shiny as jewels. I spot Nicole, a diamond wearing silver. The guy she's dancing with must be her fiancé. They're a matched pair, gleaming teeth, coiffed hair.

I expected some awkwardness, but I didn't expect my heart to race and my breathing to grow shallow like I've been thrown from my board, battered by waves, barely able to suck in a little oxygen before being tossed under again.

My gaze lands on another jewel, a vision in emerald green, only more precious than the rarest emerald on earth.

Rosie.

She's dancing with a tall, slim man who's tossing her around the dance floor without finesse, but she's laughing, looking like she's having a great time anyway. I despise him instantly.

But as I watch them, my heart rate slows, my breathing evens out. Rosie's safe, happy, even. It might sting that she's happy without me, but it's enough to know that she's thriving. That's all I want for her. I haven't forgotten that I wanted to be a part of what made her thrive, but I can live without that as long as I'm sure she's okay.

I inch toward the dance floor, wondering if it's tacky to interrupt them mid-dance. Maybe I should get a beer first, or try one of the tiny bits of puffy food that seem to be rushing around on trays.

Maybe I should stop being a coward and go talk to her.

Nicole gets to me first, with a hug and a kiss, which seems excessive since we've only actually met each other a couple of times, but whatever, it's her party, and introduces me to her fiancé.

"Congratulations," I say, even as I try to keep Rosie in my line of sight.

"Thanks. You're a friend of Rosie's?" he asks.

"And Gus is the director of horticulture here at Pacifica

Park," Nicole says, sounding as proud as if she had something to do with my promotion. "Tessa told me."

"Awesome, man," Ricky says. "This place is something else. It's making me realize we need to rethink the landscaping in our backyard. The previous owners were really into hydrangeas and our water bills were crazy this summer."

I wince. "Hydrangeas are not a Southern California-friendly flower. Have you thought about xeriscaping?"

"I haven't, but only because I have no idea what that is," Ricky says with a self-deprecating smile.

"Designing for drought. I could give you some ideas if you—"

"That's such a nice offer," Nicole breaks in, "but maybe we could talk about it later? Right now, we've got to check in with Tessa and make sure dinner is on schedule. And you—" she pushes me toward the dance floor "—should go say hi to Rosie."

I swallow. Right.

The song ends as I get within speaking distance of the most beautiful woman at the party. Her ears glitter with jewelry, her hair looks soft and touchable, her mouth is painted red. When she sees me, her eyes widen, but she smiles a little, and I relax a fraction.

The bozo she's been dancing with continues to stick to her side as she faces me full-on.

"Gus."

"Hi, Rosie." I smile at her, wishing we were alone, wishing I could say everything that's been swirling around in my head and my heart these last few days. But we're not alone and there's this big hulking guy hovering over us. I finally acknowledge him. "What's up, man?"

Rosie seems to realize the man is still there. "Oh! Jake, this is my friend, Gus. Gus, this is my little brother, Jake."

I trip a little over the word *little*, since this guy is at least six inches taller than me, and I'm not exactly short. But brother—now I put this grown man together with the kid in the graduation photo in Rosie's bedroom. I smile at him, genuinely happy to meet someone Rosie's related to. "Nice to meet you, Jake."

"Same," he says. We shake firmly, as if testing what the other is made of. Apparently we pass each other's inspections, because Jake backs off. "I'm going to check on Becca. She's tired tonight."

"Have her put her feet up," Rosie suggests.

He nods and weaves his way through the crowd.

"Do you—" I start.

"What are you—" she talks over me, then stops, laughs. I motion for her to continue. "What are you doing here, Gus?"

"I was invited by Nicole. Apparently I'm in her inner circle now. She must be really hard up for friends."

"Nicole's good at making friends. I'm glad she invited you."

"Are you?"

"Yeah. But I'm embarrassed." Her cheeks pink up on cue. "I should have been the one to invite you. I thought about it about a million times this week."

I feel my eyes widen. "You did?"

She nods and bites her lip. "I think I owe you an apology. I mean, I *do* owe you an apology."

"Hermosa, you don't owe me anything."

"I just—there's so much to tell you—and I shouldn't ask you to stick around while I figure my shit out. Even though I want to."

She says that last part quietly, but the words fill my chest with a tentative hope. "I want to hear everything. Anything. If you want me to wait, I'll wait." I step closer, slide my hand into hers. "Or maybe we can figure out some stuff together. I have things to tell you, too, you know."

She stares down at our intertwined hands. "Like what?"

"Like, I'm finally realizing I've been in a long-term relationship with this garden for a while, and I'm fully committing. I got the job."

"You did? That's wonderful." She throws her arms around me and it's kind of insane how good it feels to hold her again.

I don't let her go right away. Instead, I walk her a few steps toward the center of the dance floor. The DJ has on something slow and sultry. I slide my hands around her waist. "Will you dance with me, Rosie?"

"Of course."

I don't know what we've decided about us, exactly, but I know that as we circle the floor, our bodies are closer than just friends would be. We're no longer in fling territory, but beyond that I have no clue. Maybe it doesn't matter.

Rosie puts her cheek against my chest, and I press in closer until I can feel all of her curves nestled against me. I kiss the top of her head; silky strands of hair tickle my chin. "I missed you, hermosa."

She sighs and wriggles closer and I wish we were alone. Maybe I'll bring her back here some night to dance under the stars to an invisible orchestra, the grass dewy under our feet.

"You're a good dancer," I say as the song comes to an end. Rosie draws back to look at me.

"Really? Thanks." She makes a funny face. "You're just as good as you were in high school."

"What do you mean?"

"You don't remember?"

I shake my head.

"My sophomore year. The year we had history together. I never went to the school dances but for some reason I got talked into going to winter formal. I was so uncomfortable—it was so not like a school dance from the movies."

"They never are." I remember going to school dances with my boys, wearing aftershave and bolo ties and trying to hook up with girls who wanted nothing to do with us.

"Well, I noticed this group of boys who'd actually dressed up, and who actually danced with girls instead of just messing around with their friends. A slow song started playing that I had no intention of dancing with anyone to, but all of a sudden there you were—the cute junior from World History —and you asked me to dance and I was too surprised to say no."

"I did? I don't remember." I try to conjure up the memory, but it isn't there.

"We danced and didn't talk and when it was over you said thank you and went back to your friends like a gentleman."

"Damn. I wish I could remember that dance."

"It was the first time I ever danced with a boy. And it was almost like something out of a movie, so thanks for that." She looks at me shyly, as if embarrassed to reveal her tender little secret.

My heart swells with affection for teenage Rosie, lonely and grieving and not all that different from the Rosie that's right in front of me. "I'll dance with you anytime, if you'll have me."

"I'd like that."

Can life get any better?

At that moment the DJ announces that dinner's being served, so I guess life can get a little better; I'm suddenly starving. Rosie grabs my hand to lead me to the center table, where Nicole's holding court. I recognize her and Ricky but no one else.

We sit, since the servers are no joke setting down salads in front of every place and I understand Nicole well enough to know she's not going to be happy if her party schedule gets messed with.

"Gus, I want you to meet the rest of the bridesmaids," Rosie says, gesturing to three women sitting on her right.

Rosie seems a little nervous as she introduces me to Ophelia, Lani, and Kate, whose names I'm going to do my best to remember but who for now I label, respectfully, of course, as the blonde, the brunette, and the redhead.

They greet me with an overall coolness in their attitudes and I chalk it up to protectiveness of Rosie and move on, as Rosie greets the guys on my left and they introduce themselves in turn.

"Jamie Kendell, Ricky's cousin and best man."

"Adam O'Dowd, groomsman."

"Cory French, groomsman."

AKA the one with glasses, the one with a goatee, and the one with the sunburn. There is no way I'm going to remember all these names, but I'll try for Rosie's sake.

We're about to dig into the delicious-looking salad when Nicole snaps out a single word. "Wait!" Eight grown people freeze and turn their attention to her. "What is going on with this seating arrangement? What happened to boy-girl-boy-girl?"

"We're not in kindergarten," the brunette—Lani, I mean—says. But she gets up sheepishly, as do some of the others until we're repositioned to Nicole's liking. Now I'm between the redhead and Rosie, and glasses guy—Jamie—is next to Ophelia. The two of them start an animated conversation about the latest bakery opening in Santa Barbara's Funk Zone, so I gather that as cousins of the bride and groom they already know each other.

"Nicole doesn't mess around," I say under my breath, lest the woman hear me.

"She's the real deal," Rosie confirms. "I used to think she was a Bridezilla, but now I think of her more as Napoleon. A master of strategy."

"Intimidating. And cool," I say. Rosie grins. "And what's the deal with the bridesmaids? They seem like a tough crowd."

"They're—" Rosie struggles for the word "—determined women."

"So you fit right in."

She pushes my arm playfully. "I thought I did."

"What does that mean?"

"I guess I mean that it's kind of amazing to go through life thinking one thing about yourself and then one day realize you were completely wrong. It should be scary, but it's actually... freeing."

"What are you saying?"

The woman on my left sighs. I turn to her—Kate—and take in her rueful expression. "She's saying she wants out of the club."

"What club?"

"Kate!"

I turn back to Rosie in time to see her give Kate one of those inscrutable girl looks that I don't even pretend to be able to decipher. Then she smiles a smile I've never seen on her before. It's small but vulnerable. It makes me hope.

"I hate to admit it, but I do."

"I had a feeling," Kate says dryly. I feel like I missed the first reel of the movie.

"I'm sorry," Rosie says quietly.

"Don't be sorry, Rosie. It's okay to change your mind. It's okay to fall in love." Kate smiles, a soft, sad smile that makes me wonder who broke her heart. Then she glares at me. "But if you hurt her, you will have four very *determined* women knocking on your door. Understood?"

If being with Rosie means being accountable to her friends, it's a deal I'll gladly try to live up to. I hold up my hands in surrender. "Understood."

I'm impressed that Rosie hasn't tripped over Kate dropping the word "love." She leans across me to give Kate an awkward sort of hug. Her hair tickles my nose and I breathe her in. Suddenly, I've lost my appetite. I could live on Rosie alone.

But it seems Nicole's got the servers on a schedule, because our salad plates are whisked away and entrees placed before us. The food is gorgeous, fresh, local, but I barely taste it, brushing against Rosie's arm as often as I can, listening to the conversation at the table, trying to visualize this being the first of many meals with Rosie at my side.

By the time Nicole's parents make their obligatory speech and invite everyone to the dessert table for individual fruit tarts in every color of the rainbow, my hunger for food is sated, but my need for Rosie has only grown.

"So, what do you think of everyone?" Rosie says, when we abandon the table and grab a couple of desserts.

"Everyone's great," I say heartily. Maybe too heartily.

Rosie narrows her eyes at me. "They're not that bad," she protests.

"No, no, they're fine. Great. Fine. Just a little..."

"Boring?"

"Mostly that's Ricky's friends, I think. The girls are awesome. Nicole's a trip. Lani must be a saint to work with her every day. Ophelia, she seems cool, even though she didn't stop talking to that guy in the glasses the whole time."

"I think they're pretty good friends," Rosie says. "Convenient, since they're going to be cousins-in-law."

"Kate's a badass," I say. "You've known her since college, right?"

"Yeah. I'm lucky to still be friends with her and Nicole."

"They're lucky to be friends with you."

"Thanks."

"So, do you think anyone would miss us if I gave you an exclusive night-time private tour of the garden?"

I expect her to put up more of an argument, but she just glances around, weaves her fingers through mine. "I thought you'd never ask."

CHAPTER 34

ROSIE

This night has been surreal from the start, and the feeling that I'm in some kind of dream only intensifies the farther away from the party Gus leads me. We have our phones, but we don't use them for light. Instead we navigate in the dark, or rather, Gus leads, and I cling to his hand, trusting him to know where to go.

I've been to Pacifica Park often enough to sort of know that we're on the side farthest from the parking lot and the main office and that the Quonset hut is somewhere to the north of us, but I've never explored this part of the garden. I'm surprised when we come upon a little pond with a waterfall, a stone bench beside it. And all around us are twisty trees with thick gray trunks and curled fronds that look like something out of *Where the Wild Things Are*.

"What are those?" I ask, pointing at the wild trees.

"*Dracaena draco*," Gus answers. We're both near-whispering, even though there's no one around to disturb. Perhaps we don't want to disrupt the peace between us. "Also known as dragon tree."

"Dragon tree? Like the plant you gave me?"

"This is what it'll grow into. In twenty or thirty years."

"Really?" I'm shocked. I'd thought he'd given me a house-plant. But it turns out he gave me something that, if I take care of it, plant in the right place, will put down roots and grow into something strange and beautiful.

"It grows slowly at first. It'll stay small for a while. There's no rush."

"Oh yeah?" I'm pretty sure we're not talking about the dragon tree anymore.

"Yeah. No pressure."

"Well, no pressure is good. But it's nice to know there's a chance that it could grow into something bigger."

I can see his even white teeth as he smiles into the dark.

"Gus, you've been way too easy on me and my baggage, but I'm hoping my luck will hold out a little longer." I take a deep breath. "Will you give me a second chance to be a terrible girl-friend, who works too much and can't surf and always eats takeout?"

He grabs my other hand. "Only if you'll let me cook for you sometimes and remind you not to work too hard and surf while you sunbathe and read on the beach."

"Somehow I feel like I'm getting the better end of that bargain."

"Rosie, your so-called faults aren't really real. You say you work too much? I call you dedicated and ambitious. You can't surf? You tried, and you wear the hell out of a bathing suit, so who cares?"

I wrap my arms around Gus's waist. "You like me in a bathing suit?"

"Yeah. I also like what you're wearing tonight." He runs a finger under the strap of my dress and I shiver. The darkness presses around us like the walls of a room, giving the illusion of privacy. Still, it's unlikely any of the other guests will be wandering this far from the party. They don't have their own personal tour guide, after all.

"I'm really proud of you for going after the director job."

"I might not have tried for it if not for you. You're a good influence on me," he says, sliding closer, his hands around my waist.

"So I'm good for something, at least," I joke weakly.

"Rosie, stop. I could spend the rest of my life listing everything wonderful about you, but that would take up valuable kissing time. You're incredible. Believe it."

Maybe a week ago I wouldn't have. I would have argued and dismissed him. But now that I know I'm in love, I'm certainly not going to blame the messenger.

That's all too much to say, when all I really want to do is kiss him, so I get right to the point. "You're right. I'm awesome."

He chuckles. "Exactly."

"Not that I mind you telling me." I'll try to be better at hearing my strengths instead of mentally replacing them with my faults.

"Naturally."

"I don't mind you kissing me, either," I say, suddenly shy to bridge the physical distance myself.

"You want me to kiss you?" he asks, voice low and deep and the exact tenor to make my spine quiver like a plucked guitar string.

"Yes."

He obliges me by softly sealing his lips to mine. It's so damn good I could cry. I lick into his mouth, his familiar taste like coming home, then suck on the tip of his tongue. Gus groans, and suddenly our romantic kiss turns scorching hot.

We stumble together over to the bench where he pulls me down on top of him, straddling his waist. I'm reminded of that one time in his truck, but this is better, because there's no steering wheel in the way. His hands come around to cup my ass, and I grind down onto him, a bit flummoxed as to how he's going to get inside me considering his formal attire.

We stop sticking our tongues down each other's throats long enough to push his suit jacket off together, then he unbuckles his belt while I adjust my dress. He doesn't bother getting his trousers off, just pulls his dick out, hot and heavy in his hand. I'm glad I skipped the Spanx and went with regular black underwear; it's easy to push the fabric aside and slide straight onto him. Liquid pleasure flows through my veins as he stretches and fills me.

We don't talk about the fact that we're not using a condom, but it feels right. It feels amazing, actually, him bare inside me. There's nothing separating us. Everywhere else we're separated by the heavy fabric of our ridiculous fancy clothes.

Gus kneads my breasts through my dress and bra. I'd like to tear the damn things off, but I have enough presence of mind to know that's a really bad idea. I push his shirt up as far as it will go, run my hands over his stomach, the ridges of his abs made more prominent by his position and the physicality with which he's moving beneath me. He pushes his hips up and I grind myself down and soon we've got a rhythm going that's building toward somewhere very good.

I can't see his face well in the light, but I can tell his hair is flopping down over his forehead and his mouth is open and his eyes are dark. He's beautiful.

My orgasm's bearing down on me, and I scramble to hold onto him, needing the grounding of his shoulders beneath my fingers as I pant as silently as I can through it, gripping him for dear life, every sound ten times as loud in the darkness, the sweet scent of the earth filling my nose as my whole body shakes and spasms around the point of pleasure that joins us together.

"Yes," I hiss as I start to come down. "Gus."

When I say his name he grips my waist harder and he slams

me down one more time. I can feel him shudder as he empties himself inside me. It's warm and intimate and I'm infused with a possessive afterglow. He's the first man I've let come inside me without a condom.

I slump over him as his arms come around my back, holding me to him. We're both quiet, shaking through the aftershocks until the night silence returns, and I make a discovery. Having sex without a condom is fucking awesome, and also fucking messy. A stickiness spreads between us, and I don't want to shift for fear of ruining any of our clothes more than they've already been ruined.

"I don't suppose you have such a thing as a handkerchief on you?" I ask, feeling prissy and awkward.

Gus shifts me to one side, and digs around in his trouser pocket. "Will this do?" He holds up a bandana, clean and neatly folded.

I can't help but kiss him enthusiastically in response. What woman doesn't appreciate a well-prepared man? He laughs. "I always carry one."

"You and Ricky have more in common than you might think." I use the proffered fabric to clean us both up as best I can. I move off Gus's lap so he can reassemble himself, but I don't go far, curling up against his side. He puts an arm around me and I lean my head on his shoulder.

Maybe it's the darkness and the fact that I can't see his face and he can't see mine, but I feel brave enough to say what was running through my mind the entire time he was inside me.

Still, I have to take a calming breath. I've never said this to anyone before and it's slightly terrifying. "Gus?"

"Yes, Rosie?"

"I know we agreed no pressure and all that, but is it okay if I tell you that I love you?"

The hand that's stroking up and down the bare skin of my

arm stills. I hold my breath. "Hermosa. It's more than fucking okay. I love you, too."

My chest tightens with relief, with love, with a thousand emotions all tumbling inside me. I turn my head toward him, bury my face in his neck, and say it again. "I love you." I sigh into his warm skin and he kisses my hair. Being this close to him feels like a gift, something precious I'm finally allowing myself to have.

We just sit like that for a while. I'm warm everywhere my body touches his. I'd never want to leave this moment except I know that we have so many amazing moments in store for us now that I'm finally brave enough to ask for them.

"Do you think the party's still going on?" I ask, regretting my instinct to do the right thing and make sure Nicole's night has gone as well as she wanted it to.

"Probably," Gus says. He pulls something else out of those apparently voluminous pockets of his. The flare of light from his cell phone screen seems obscene now that I'm accustomed to the darkness. "It's almost eleven."

"Shit." We've been gone for a while. I only hope that Nicole is having such an amazing time she hasn't realized I've been missing. "I guess we should—"

Gus's phone rings, breaking into my thoughts. The number that comes up is local, but doesn't have a name attached. I glance at it idly, figuring it's spam, but then I recognize it. "Wait, that's my brother's number."

Gus answers immediately. "Hello?"

I can hear the tenor of my brother's voice, stressed, through the speaker. He's asking for me and Gus hands over the phone without a word.

"Jake?"

"There's something wrong with Becca. She says she's having some pretty bad pain. I don't know what to do." The fear in

Jake's voice goes right to my core, but I know I have to stay calm for his sake.

"Where are you?"

"The parking lot. She wanted to leave an hour ago, but I was having fun. We just started back to the car when she doubled over. Should I take her to the hospital?"

"Let me come take a look, okay?"

"Hurry, Rosie."

CHAPTER 35

ROSIE

I fly off the bench. "Becca's not well. Jake's got her in the parking lot and I need to go check on her. Can you take me there?"

"Follow me." Gus uses his light and I grab my purse. I find my phone, switched to silent, and spot three missed calls from Jake. He must have called Nicole to get Gus's number. I push away my nausea when I realize that I was having sex with Gus when my brother and his pregnant fiancée needed me.

Gus pulls me along the dark garden paths as fast as he can. I'm completely turned around, but Gus forges on confidently. He'll get me there.

Suddenly, we're back at the main office. He leads me through a small side gate and we find ourselves in the parking lot. I see Jake's SUV and him pacing next to it.

"Hey," I say when I get close enough to see Becca lying in the passenger seat, rubbing her distended stomach. "What's going on, Becca?"

"She's in pain!" Jake says before his fiancée can answer. "Do something, please!"

I give Jake a look that has him snapping his mouth into a flat line and turn back to Becca. She looks pale, with shadows under her eyes and a groove between her eyebrows. "Can you tell me how you're feeling?"

"I've been tired all day. Crampy. I didn't want to go out tonight but I knew Nicole and Ricky really wanted us to be here."

"When did the pain start?"

"Like an hour ago? Just like, really bad cramps. But I'm only thirty-five weeks."

"It could be Braxton Hicks. Did you call your OB?"

"I left a message with the service but they haven't called me back yet," Jake says. Tension radiates off of him and I spare a thought for how worried he must be.

"Okay. Keep your phone handy." I wish I had my stethoscope, but I hold Becca's wrist gently and take her pulse. It's a little fast, but strong.

"Can I do something?" Gus asks quietly.

"A bottle of water would be good," I say. He nods and disappears.

"Okay, Bec." I smile at her with confidence I don't feel. She's not Mom, but she is my family, and I'm not going to let her down. I have to be Dr. Snyder right now. I can't hide from this. I can't be afraid.

"Oh, ouch." Becca grabs her side and tenses up. I keep count and it's twenty seconds before she relaxes again. That's an intense contraction, and could be an indicator that she's going into labor.

"You're going to be fine, Becca. I think that Jake needs to drive us to the hospital, just to get you checked out. You might be dehydrated and it might be false labor. I'm going to stay with you the entire time."

"Thanks, Rosie." Becca's voice is strong, just like she is.

Gus returns with two water bottles from the bar and my wrap that I left on the table. He must have run the entire way there and back. I give him a grateful smile.

"I told Nicole we had to leave. She's cool," Gus says briefly. "Thanks."

I give Becca water and make her take a small sip. The men are hovering. The best thing I can do for them is to give them something to do.

"Jake, give me your phone. I'm going to try to reach your doctor, while you drive us to my hospital. If I can't reach them, I'll call ahead and make sure they know to expect us."

Jake thrusts the phone at me and climbs into the driver's seat. I turn to Gus.

"Hey. I'm going to go with them."

"Of course." He gives me an encouraging smile. "Everything is going to be fine."

"That's usually my line." Him saying it makes me feel better, anyway.

"Do you want me to come with you?"

"No sense in us both having to come back for our cars. Why don't you go home. I'll call you later."

"Yeah, okay." He doesn't look super happy about it.

"Hey, I have to go to work now," I say softly. "But I'll come back."

He gives me a quick kiss. "I know."

Jake's been quiet this whole time, but his impatience wins out and he growls, "Come on, Rosie." I hop in the car and watch Gus disappear into the darkness behind us.

Jake drives just over the speed limit and gets on the freeway, then lets out a groan. "What the fuck?"

We join a line of cars stopped on the 101. Bumper-to-bumper traffic at nearly midnight on a Saturday night? God, I hate California sometimes.

"There must be an accident," Becca says, and she lets out a small moan.

"Breathe, sweetie," I say. Jake's face is a granite ode to worry. I honestly don't know what to do. Should we get off the freeway? Should we call an ambulance? If Becca's going into labor, and all signs point to yes, even though she's uncomfortable we have time before anything major is going to happen. Probably.

But what if she has complications? What if there's something wrong and I don't catch it? What if—

Jake's phone rings, and I'm about to answer it but he punches a button on the steering wheel and the entire car floods with sound. "This is Dr. Chadha. What's going on, guys?"

I don't know Dr. Chadha personally, but I've heard her name around the hospital. I usually give the obstetrics department a wide berth, so to speak, so it's not surprising we haven't crossed paths before.

"Hi, it's Becca. I'm, uh, having contractions. I think?" Her voice is a tad breathy and I rub her shoulder from the back seat. "Jake and I were at a party and now we're in the car and we're stuck in traffic in Carpinteria and—"

Dr. Chadha, apparently aware of Becca's verbose tendencies, interrupts her to ask the same questions I did about the onset of the symptoms, frequency and duration of the contractions.

Becca starts to answer, but she's hit by another wave of pain and swallows down a shocked gasp. Jake stays quiet but he's white knuckling the steering wheel as we inch forward, still about a mile from the next exit.

It's time for me to step in.

"Dr. Chadha? This is Rosie Snyder, I'm a doctor at VMH. I'm here with Becca and Jake—he's my brother—"

"Oh, you're the doctor sister!" Dr. Chadha exclaims. "Wish we were meeting under different circumstances. Jake's told me a lot about you."

Apparently Jake talks about me, just not to me. Whatever. Not the most important thing at the moment.

"Yeah, so the thing is, these could be Braxton Hicks, but

they do seem to be getting longer, stronger, and closer together."

"That's the magic formula," she agrees merrily. "You guys better come into the hospital. I'll call ahead so they're expecting you."

"It might take us a while to get there. Becca doesn't have any complications that we need to worry about, does she?"

"Nope. She's perfect, the baby's in a good position. First-time labor usually isn't that quick so I'd say you have plenty of time to get here."

I relax a degree. She's right. I need to trust my instincts. Just because something could go wrong doesn't mean it will.

"Sounds good. Thanks, Doctor."

"Becca, you hang in there," Dr. Chadha says firmly. "If you're in labor, it just means that baby's anxious to meet you. Everything's going to be fine."

I think she's going to hang up, but she adds, "And Jake, stop freaking out. I can sense you silently going crazy all the way here in Oxnard. Chill, dude."

Jake lets out a shaky laugh. "Thanks, Dr. Chadha," he says, sounding a little less uptight.

Then she does hang up, and a bit later the traffic starts flowing. Becca keeps having contractions every few minutes, and Jake focuses on driving safely. I hold Becca's hand from the back seat.

Becca, for once, doesn't seem to feel like talking much, so I talk instead. "It was a nice party. I hope Nicole had fun."

"You and Gus missed most of it," Jake says shortly.

I laugh a little at the little brother officiousness in his tone, given everything else that's going on. "I was hoping nobody would notice. I guess we did."

"What's going on with you two?" Becca asks.

"We're..." I think about the right word to describe what we are. We went from a fling to broken up to having hot semi-public sex in three weeks. We're in love and I can't imagine that changing anytime soon. "...together."

Becca makes a soft sound of happiness. Jake scowls. "This is the guy that works at Pacifica Park?"

I lift my eyebrows, surprised that my car-mechanic brother cares if my boyfriend has a blue-collar job. "He's the director of horticulture, if you must know." Not that I'd care if he cut lawns and raked leaves all day.

"Actually, we went to high school together, but we only met again a few weeks ago." I say this to Becca, not my stupid brother.

"How romantic," she sighs, then moans, and pants for about thirty seconds. "Fuck. You know, intellectually, I knew this part was going to hurt, but I didn't think it was going to hurt this much."

"You're doing amazing." I push away the thread of fear that it shouldn't hurt this much this soon. But since I've never given birth and have in fact avoided most birthing-related medicine as much as possible in my career, I have to rely on my rudimentary knowledge that this is, in fact, normal.

Jake's clearly worried enough for both of us, because he steps on the gas even harder and all of a sudden we're only two exits from the hospital.

"Thanks for being here," Becca says.

"Of course." I squeeze her hand. "What good is having a doctor in the family if you can't use them in emergencies? Not that this is an emergency, exactly—"

Becca interrupts me with another gasp. "Um. Baby? I think my water just broke. Or I just peed. Not sure."

I crane my neck, and yes, even in the dark and given Becca's black clothes, I can see liquid dripping and soaking the car seat upholstery. For one horrible second lasting the length of a heartbeat, I see blood. Then I blink and my vision clears. This is not a drill. Becca's in labor.

"Your car's getting all yucky." Becca sounds on the verge of tears.

"Fuck the car." Jake sounds together, if tense.

I scan the back seat for something to soak up the fluid, remembering I need to check to see if it's clear or if the baby's meconium has gotten into the amniotic fluid. My brother is a clean freak and his back seat is completely empty.

"Jesus, Jake, you don't have anything back here. Don't you ever eat takeout?"

"I don't think McDonald's napkins are going to do much in this situation," he says dryly.

"Good point."

Becca wails again, and I'm relieved when we finally get off the freeway and zoom through a couple of lights to get to the hospital. I direct Jake to the emergency entrance, where we'll get the fastest response at this time of night.

"I'll take her in, get her where she needs to be," I say, my heart rate steadying now that we're on the familiar hospital grounds. "You park and call me and I'll let you know where to meet us."

He nods, kisses Becca briefly, and helps her out of the car before speeding off.

Becca's wheezing and her dress is soaked, but there doesn't seem to be any meconium in the fluid on the seat, so that's a good thing. In fact, everything about this is textbook except for the fact that she's a month early and things seem to be progressing really fast.

I murmur useless motivational phrases as we get inside and I use my doctor privileges to get Becca admitted immediately into a private room in the OB ward, which is thankfully not very busy at the moment. Jake finds us a few minutes later, while Becca's changing into a gown in the bathroom.

"Where is she?" His face is tight, and he's shed his jacket and tie.

"Changing. She's going to be fine. She's strong. Everything's good. It's just going fast."

"Her mom was only in labor for like three hours with her," Jake says hoarsely. "I told her it could be the same with her."

"Well, that explains it," I say, vaguely recalling that sometimes quick labor runs in families. "You two might have mentioned that."

"I was scared. I'm still scared," Jake says quietly. The Snyders haven't been huggers until recently, but I go to my brother, put an arm around him.

"I know. It's okay to be scared. You love her. It makes sense. But she's doing well. You have excellent care here. You're going to be a dad soon."

"Wow." He laughs a little. "Wild, huh?"

"Wild. But brilliant. You're going to do great."

"Thanks. And thanks for being here. Thanks for... everything."

My throat tightens. I want to tell him I love him, but somehow it's too much. Instead I hug him harder. He hugs me back and we don't have to say anything else at all.

When Becca's settled and the nurse has given her an IV and checked her, she's declared five centimeters dilated already. It could be a few hours or a few minutes more, so I slip out to call Gus.

I'm only planning on leaving him a message but he picks up on the second ring.

"Hey." He doesn't sound like he was asleep.

"Hey. I'm at the hospital. Becca's having the baby. It could be a while yet, but I wanted to let you know."

"Thanks. I was worried."

I smile. Gus has only just met Jake and Becca, but he cares about them, because they're my family. "I'm going to stay, but I'll let you know if there are any developments. And maybe tomorrow..."

"I'll keep it free."

"Do that."

"Goodnight, Rosie."

"Goodnight, Gus." Before I lose my nerve, I add, "I love you," then hang up before he can say it back.

* * *

I should be tired, but I'm too jittery to feel exhausted. This is Jake and Becca's time, and I don't really need to be here, but since I'd have to call a car to get home, I decide to stay. They're not going to need me for any medical reason now that Dr. Chadha's en route, but maybe there's something I can do just because I'm family.

Jake gives me his phone and asks me to let Becca's parents know she's in labor, so I make a phone call to a very sleepy, surprised Mrs. Adams.

"But she's only thirty-five weeks," she says after I explain what's going on.

"The baby decided to come early, apparently."

"Isn't that bad?"

"Well, depending on the baby's size and weight, they might want to keep her in the NICU for a few days—"

"The NICU?" Her voice rises with fright.

"Listen, Mrs. Adams, there's nothing to worry about right now. Jake just wanted to make sure you knew what was going on. We'll get back in touch when we know more."

"All right, but—"

My attention is caught by Jake appearing at the door, a dazed look on his face.

"What?" I ask, forgetting about Mrs. Adams.

"She's here," Jake says. "Six pounds even. Nineteen inches."

"Oh my God! That was the fastest delivery ever," I say, and then have to hold the phone away from my ear as Mrs. Adams screeches. I thrust the phone at Jake, who takes it and starts to explain to Becca's mom that her granddaughter was born in record time.

I laugh, giddy with joy and relief. Jake's a dad. I'm an aunt. I can't wait to meet her. I can't wait to tell Gus about this. I can't wait for—well, for everything that life has in store for us.

CHAPTER 36
GUS

I don't know how I manage to get to sleep after Rosie calls me to tell me her niece has been born, but I do, and I'm still sleeping when Rosie taps on the sliding glass door to my bedroom, startling me out of a dream that involved her and me making out on a surfboard in the middle of the ocean.

I never thought of myself as much of an exhibitionist, but since I met Rosie, all I can think about is making love to her in nature, so maybe there's something there.

I jump out of bed and unlock the door. Rosie's beaming. I've never seen her smile so hard. It's a good look on her. She looks young and happy.

God. I love her so much it's a little scary. I've only known the girl for three weeks. Then again, I've technically known her since I was fifteen. So maybe it's not rushing things to want her to abandon her sad little condo and move in with me. I shelve that thought as I hug her, then pull her onto bed with me. She's no longer in her flirty little party dress, which is a shame, but the yoga pants she's wearing hug her ass like a dream, so I'm not complaining.

She laughs as I pull the covers over us. "I'm still wearing my shoes."

"Don't care."

She shucks them off, then climbs back in and settles into the curve of my arms like she belongs there, which, of course, she does.

"Everything okay?" I ask, breathing in the scent of her hair greedily.

"Becca's doing great. Baby's doing great. They think it's possible they messed up on the due date a little bit, because she's really not presenting like a preemie. They took her to the NICU as a precaution, then brought her right back and she's been with Becca ever since."

"That's amazing."

"Jake's kind of in shock—it all happened so fast—but he's good."

"And how are you?"

"I'm—" she snuggles closer to me "—exhausted. But happy. The baby is so cute, they let me hold her, and you'll never guess what they named her?"

"Umm…" I think about Rosie and her mother, Iris. "Dahlia? Lily? Euphorbia?"

"Euphorbia? No. But you're not far off. Daisy. That was the name my mom had picked out for my sister." She hesitates over the word only slightly, and her mood picks right back up again. "Isn't that sweet? Baby Daisy."

"That's the perfect name." I entertain brief thoughts of little brown-haired babies with Rosie's big eyes and wonder if she's dedicated to carrying on the family naming tradition. If we have a boy, will he be named Sage? Honestly, whatever she wants is fine by me.

Rosie yawns and burrows closer. "I'm so tired. I need a vacation from my vacation."

I freeze. "Does that mean you're going back to work Monday?" I'm aware there's some trepidation in my voice. I know we can make this work, but we've never attempted it while she was doing her full-on doctor thing before.

She sits up and looks at me. "Don't *you* have to work Monday?"

I really, really want to suggest we play hooky. But I actually have work to do and I actually want to do that work. I sink back against the pillows. "Yeah, I do."

She kisses me. "So we'll both go to work. And after work, I'll come over here. We'll have dinner. Then we'll have sex. We'll sleep together all night long. And the next day we'll do it all over again."

I grin. "Sounds like a plan."

"And we still have today," she reminds me. "The last day of our fling."

"Your last fling." I laugh. "Thank God."

"Yours too."

"I'm counting on it."

EPILOGUE
ROSIE

"I'm so glad we're finally doing this," Gus's mom, Sandra, says to me as we board the boat bound for Anacapa Island. It's a stunningly clear January day. The water looks cold, but the air is comfortable. We can always count on a few higher-than-average temps in January, and today is perfect for a boat trip.

"Best Christmas present ever, Rosie," Gus's dad agrees.

"I'm glad we found a date that worked for everyone." Scheduling the Cuevases and the Snyders would have been bad enough, but we added in Nicole and Ricky, Snyders-by-extension, and the calendar got really complicated.

But we all made it. Becca looks radiant with Daisy bundled close to her chest. The three-month-old has been nursing nonstop and has almost doubled her birth weight. Jake hovers over them, taller than everyone else by a head, and still taciturn, except when he's cooing at his daughter like the besotted father he is.

"How long does it take to get there?" Nicole asks, looking fashionable in a green Patagonia windbreaker she no doubt purchased for this exact outing.

"About an hour and a half," Ricky says. He's done his

research and has already had one conversation with the captain about the safety features of the boat.

I dutifully put on my life jacket and help Eddie, Gus's nephew, put his on. His moms, Jess and Carla, are trying to herd everyone to the bow of the boat for a group picture.

I hang back once I'm sure that Eddie's got his jacket on and understands the instructions to stay away from the sides of the boat. Everyone hums with excitement over our excursion, but I just need a minute.

I don't see Gus with the others, and then I realize he's materialized at my side. He grabs my hand, kisses my hair in a gesture that I've come to cherish. He loves my hair, he's told me about a zillion times. We've had some ups and downs in the last few months, but every day has honestly been better than the day before.

"Everything okay?" he asks. He's gotten frighteningly good at reading me.

"Yeah. Look at everyone." Our families are laughing and talking and Jess is probably having less success organizing them for a picture than she does with her students.

"What about them?"

"This time last year, I didn't have anyone. Well, just Jake. But I didn't even know he had a girlfriend. Now I have a sister-in-law and a niece and you guys and—it's a lot."

"I know. Just so you know, we're really happy to have you in the family."

"Thanks."

"Although you might not think it's so great to be in with the Cuevases after my mom hints for the fiftieth time that we should get married."

"What? She's never said anything to me."

"Not yet. But she will."

"I can handle it."

"You can handle anything." Gus kisses me. "But please don't tell her you were in something called the Never a Bride Club."

"Hey, I'm still in the club—honorary member only."

"That's good to hear," Gus says. "Just don't say I didn't warn you."

"Hey, you two, you're holding up the picture," Jess calls.

Gus grabs my hand and we thread our way up the boat. The sun is bright and the engines hum. Gus thrusts me into the front of the group, sandwiching himself between me and Carla, never letting go of my hand. Jess has gotten one of the boat's crew, some gangly kid, to take the picture.

"Say 'Anacapa!'" Jess yells. We comply and the kid takes about a million pictures.

"Okay, I think we got it," Jess waves and the kid hands back over the phone.

"Wow, we're a good looking group," Gus says, looking over her shoulder at the shot.

"Just imagine how cute your and Rosie's babies would be," Sandra says.

"Mom!"

I laugh, startled. Okay, so she skipped the marriage stuff and went straight to babies.

"What? Eddie and Daisy need cousins."

"Jesus, Mom."

I look at Gus. His cheeks are stained red and he's avoiding my eyes. But the scary thing is, thinking about having a baby with him isn't scary at all. We're not ready yet, and whenever it happens, it's going to be hard with both of us working. But we'll figure it out. And our baby will have cousins, and grandparents, and aunts and uncles. It will have a family. That baby will be so loved.

"You know what, Sandra? You're right. Eddie and Daisy do need more cousins. Give us a little while, okay?"

She grins with sly satisfaction at my answer, then the boat

starts to pull away from the dock and everyone gets wound up about our trip again.

Gus shakes his head. "Sorry about that."

"No, it's okay. I guess the marriage thing is implied if she thinks we should have babies."

"Did you mean that? What you said to her?"

"No pressure or anything, but, yeah."

He smiles. "No pressure."

And we sail off toward the future.

* * *

Thank you so much for reading *Can't Help Falling in Love!*

Scan this code to download a FREE Never a Bride story to learn how Nicole and Ricky began their love affair!

Thanks for being a part of the world of the Never a Brides!

xoxo,

Libby

ACKNOWLEDGMENTS

Books are written solo and brought to the world by a whole passel of people. Thank you to those whose brains I picked relentlessly and who never complained of having to explain the same things over and over to me: Thomas Baker-Rabe, Anna Bower, Daniel Zweier, and Dr. Julie Lemieux. Their help was invaluable and any mistakes are mine.

Thanks to my biggest cheerleaders, plot doctors, and dear friends: Monique St. Paul, Lena Eson Roe, Annette Nauraine, Kate Kettler, Isabel Morin, and the wonderful group of writers that make up the Connecticut Chapter of Romance Writers of America and the virtual community of romance writers whose enthusiasm and encouragement have made this entire series possible.

Huge thank you to the expertise of my editing and design team: Sue Khodarahmi, Brian Calvert of Calvert Illustrations, and Dylan Osborn. This book is beautiful because of you.

Special thanks to all the women in my family. You're my best examples of lives well lived.

To my husband and sons, you are my inspiration and my pride. I'm a writer because I want to show you that creativity matters, that stories are worth telling, that you can change the world by doing something you love.

ABOUT THE AUTHOR

Libby Waterford is the author of the Sawyer's Cove: The Reboot and the Never a Bride series. She's obsessed with her pollinator garden, DIY fermentation, and writing swoony first kisses and hopeful happily ever afters. Her steamy contemporary romances mix witty banter and all the feels with a solid dollop of good old-fashioned sexual tension. Libby wrangles her two ever-growing sons and a husband in Fairfield County, Connecticut.

Get a free story at libbywaterford.com and email her at libby@libbywaterford.com.

facebook.com/LibbyWaterford

instagram.com/libbywritesromance

bookbub.com/authors/libby-waterford

goodreads.com/libbywaterford

amazon.com/author/libbywaterford

tiktok.com/@libbywaterfordauthor